25

BRIE'S SUBMISSION

Beneath the Flames

Red Phoenix

Beneath the Flames:
Brie's Submission Book 25

Cover by Shanoff Designs
Formatted by BB Books
Phoenix symbol by Nicole Delfs

Dedication

Wow, this book!!!

I won't lie, I was intimidated about writing this book even before I began. I had two heavy hitters I had to write about and both of them were going to share personal things I was unsure of. Marquis Gray and Master Nosh are deep thinkers, way deeper than me, so I was unsure if I could do either of them justice.

I basically had to give the book over to my muses and trust they would help me to navigate each of their stories—and oh my, what stories they had to share with us!

There are a LOT of things revealed in this book, some that have been brewing for years, my friends. It was fun to finally share them with you and naturally it will change the course of some of these people's lives, but never fear. Every one of them is learning and growing into who they are meant to be.

So a huge shout out to my muses. Without them, this book would never have been written. It was way out of my comfort zone, but exactly what all of us needed.

I have to thank my editor, KH Koehler. She knew starting in that I didn't have a lot of time to write it because of difficulties happening in my life behind the scenes. She had my back, as she always does, and pointed out issues as they arose so I could quickly rectify them and move on. She went above and beyond to make my words sing.

MrRed was amazing. He never doubted I would bring the story to life and supported me with not only inspiration, but by taking care of everything in our daily lives so I could concentrate solely on this book.

Kennia believed I could do the impossible, her encouragement meant the world to me.

My sweet proofers Becki, Brenda and Marilyn took on the challenge of my crazy schedule and I can't thank them enough!

Big hugs go to Pippa Jayne for giving so much of herself every time she narrates another part of Brie's journey.

Thank you, Amanda Gallegos, for sharing the Brie joke in Friends of Red Phoenix that was added to the story.

YOU, my dear fans, are incredibly important to me. I know I would be nothing without you, but it's so much more than that. I love hearing from you, I love getting to meet you, I love hanging with you in my reader group, because your love of my books makes this journey so dang fun. Please know the important role you play in my life.

I am so very grateful.

Much love ~Red

SIGN UP FOR MY NEWSLETTER
HERE FOR THE LATEST RED
PHOENIX UPDATES

FOLLOW ME ON INSTAGRAM
INSTAGRAM.COM/REDPHOENIXAUTHOR

SALES, GIVEAWAYS, NEW
RELEASES, PREORDER LINKS, AND
MORE!
SIGN UP HERE
REDPHOENIXAUTHOR.COM/NEWSLETTER-
SIGNUP

CONTENTS

Pins and Needles

I *believe I may be responsible for Greg Holloway's death…*
Marquis Gray's text played over and over in Brie's mind, but she was unable to believe it. Of all the people she knew, Marquis was the last person she would have suspected of ending the life of another person.

Sir reached over and took his phone from her. "Do not concern yourself with Gray's message."

"But Sir…" she whimpered.

He stated firmly, "Gray's words were not meant for you."

Brie let out an anxious sigh.

"At this point, neither of us understands the context of this text. I will reach out to him once we get home."

After the suffering she'd endured during her captivity, the incredible balloon ride above the Santa Ynez Mountains had given Brie a new perspective. She'd walked away from the experience ready to embrace her life without the fears of her past holding her back.

But after seeing Marquis's confession, she'd been

shaken to her core and felt the darkness starting to creep back into her soul…

Sensing a change in her, Sir pulled to the side of the road and shut off the car. Turning to face her, he commanded, "Look at me, babygirl."

When she met Sir's gaze, he cupped her cheek in his hand. "Do *not* dwell on his words."

Brie frowned, tears pricking her eyes. "I'm worried about him, Sir…"

His eyes softened. "I understand. However, worrying is a waste of your energy."

She nodded, but her bottom lip trembled as an errant tear rolled down her cheek. How could she not worry about Marquis Gray? A desire to protect others from Greg Holloway had pushed one of the most respected men in the community to act, and now his life would be ruined because of it.

Looking deep into Brie's eyes, Sir told her, "I want you to listen to me carefully. Every single time you find yourself worrying about Gray, I want you to send him positive thoughts and let the concern go. By doing this consistently, you will acknowledge your concern without letting it have control over you. If you are diligent, those errant thoughts won't have any power over you." He stroked her cheek lovingly. "You have made too much progress to allow anything to derail you now, babygirl."

A smile of understanding slowly spread across her face, realizing he was right. It would be easy to fall back into despair but allowing that to happen wouldn't benefit Marquis and would be harmful to her. But if Brie consciously sent him positive thoughts, it might make a difference to Marquis, and would certainly ease her aching heart.

"That is wonderful advice, Sir."

He smiled as he turned on the car. She stared out of the car window to take in the breathtaking scenery of the coastline on the drive to his uncle's house to pick up the children.

Each time Marquis came to mind, she closed her eyes and sent him good thoughts and positive energy. She felt an inner reset whenever she did it.

Glancing at Sir, Brie felt deeply grateful for his timely advice.

Hours later, when Sir pulled the car into their driveway, Brie was crestfallen to see that their house was swarming with reporters. It appeared that there was renewed interest in the case since Holloway's mysterious death.

Fortunately, Hope was fast asleep in the car, having spent the day entertained by her cousin Jonathan. Brie quickly covered both children with blankets so the reporters couldn't take photos of the children as they pulled into the garage.

Once they were inside the house, Sir took their daughter upstairs to finish her nap. Brie laid a blanket out on the floor, setting Antony on it. When Sir returned downstairs, he nodded to Brie as he headed straight into his office, shutting the door behind him.

Brie frowned, concerned about what Marquis would

confess to Sir. Keeping her promise to her Master, she dutifully closed her eyes and sent both Marquis and Celestia positive thoughts before she joined Antony on the floor.

Her little boy gave her a dimpled grin and scooched on his stomach to get closer to her, a look of pure joy on his face. Brie was touched by his devotion and leaned forward to rub noses with him.

Sharing in his innocent joy seemed to overshadow everything else and she lost herself in the moment, which is why she was startled by the sound of Sir throwing open his office door.

Brie gazed up at him hoping to see a look of relief on Sir's face after finishing his phone call with Marquis. Her heart skipped a beat when she saw his grave expression.

"Gray deeply regrets causing you unnecessary pain."

Brie swooped Antony into her arms, holding him tight against her chest. "Did he explain what happened?"

He shook his head.

Fear crept into Brie's heart again when she asked, "Do you think Marquis Gray might go to jail for this?"

"I honestly don't know," Sir answered somberly.

Closing her eyes, Brie squeezed Antony tighter.

"Gray refuses to explain himself but stated several times that he regrets that you saw his text." Pausing for a moment, Sir added, "He seems to be in a very dark place."

"Poor Marquis…" she whimpered, gutted that the esteemed trainer was suffering because of that evil man. "Should we visit him, Sir?"

He shook his head. "I spoke to Celestia after my

conversation with Gray. She says we should wait until he calls on us."

"Celestia must be worried out of her mind," Brie lamented. "This situation is so unlike Marquis Gray."

Sir nodded in agreement. "Celestia insists that Marquis is a man of the highest integrity, and she fully supports whatever decision he may have made concerning Holloway."

Brie looked up at him in surprise. "So, even she doesn't know what he's done?"

"It doesn't appear so. However, Celestia is steadfast in her loyalty and confidence in him." Sir held out his hand to Brie, helping her to her feet before wrapping his arms around her waist. "Whatever Gray's actions and intentions were, they have no bearing on you, babygirl."

Brie sighed as she laid her head against his chest. "Knowing Marquis is struggling hurts my heart."

"And what are you going to do about it?" he prompted.

Closing her eyes, she replied, "I am sending him good thoughts and letting it go."

Sir kissed the top of her head. "Good girl. Your distress would only compound Gray's suffering if he knew."

Hearing a commotion outside, Sir let her go and went to the front window. Growling in disgust as he stared at the reporters, he said, "Ever since the announcement of Holloway's death, their numbers seem to keep growing…"

That night, Brie lay in Sir's arms, exhausted by the incredible highs and lows of the day. To go from the exhilaration of the balloon ride and the insights it provided to the darkness of Marquis Gray's confession was completely disorienting.

Although Brie could control her thoughts while awake, sleep turned out to be a different matter. She tossed and turned all night, unable to find rest. When it finally came in the wee hours of the morning, she quickly woke up screaming.

"Shh…babygirl," Sir commanded softly, enfolding her in his embrace. "You're safe."

Brie instantly relaxed. Turning to face him, she could not stop the tears from rolling down her cheeks and onto her pillow.

"What were you dreaming about?"

Her bottom lip trembled uncontrollably. "I don't know…"

Holding her tighter, he said in a soothing voice. "Whenever we dream, the subconscious seeks to process the emotions of the day. It's understandable that it is struggling right now, but there is nothing for you to be afraid of."

She nodded, comforted by his words and the protective strength of his embrace.

"What would help you to sleep?"

Brie stared at him in the dark, only able to see the faintest details of his face. "You, Sir. I need to feel you deep inside of me."

The fear caused by the unknown nightmare disappeared the moment he moved under the sheets and took Brie's hand. She felt butterflies when he placed it on his shaft.

Scooting closer to him, she wrapped her fingers around his cock and felt it harden with each stroke of her hand. Making him hard was empowering and made her focus her thoughts solely on him.

Sir reached under the covers and lightly brushed her mound with his fingers. She instinctively opened her legs more, craving his erotic touch.

Her pussy contracted in pleasure when he rubbed his finger against her clit. She moaned softly, momentarily distracted, but quickly returned to stroking his rigid shaft.

"My cock worships you, téa," he murmured huskily.

She smiled at him before disappearing under the sheets. "And I worship your cock, Master…"

Brie tightened her grip as she slowed her strokes and was rewarded when she felt his cock dripping with precome. She encased the smooth skin of the head of his shaft with her lips to taste his desire with her tongue. It was intoxicating and she purred in delight.

Sir guided her body into a new position so he would have free access to her pussy while she sucked his cock. Having him tease her clit with his fingers made it difficult for Brie to concentrate, but she relished the challenge, matching her movements with the rhythm of his, the experience heightening her state of arousal.

Brie was entranced with the feel of him in her mouth

and swirled her tongue around the rim of the head of his cock as if he were a giant lollipop. Knowing he liked the feel of her teeth, she grazed the sensitive skin with her teeth and heard his groan of approval. Pleasuring him in this way connected her to Sir on a different level, and she found it was easy to lose herself in the intimacy of that connection.

When he started rubbing her clit more vigorously, she arched her back, spreading her legs to give him full access.

Brie needed more and opened her mouth wider, taking his cock slowly down her throat. There was something primal and erotic about deep-throating him while he skillfully teased her aching pussy.

When Sir slowly thrust his cock down her throat, her hips began to buck of their own accord in response, announcing her imminent release.

He pulled his hand away, murmuring, "Not yet…"

Brie shuddered, forcing herself back from the edge of her oncoming climax.

"Good girl," he praised her huskily, returning his attention to her clit. "I want this orgasm to overwhelm your senses."

Knowing his intent, Brie was even more focused on his every touch. Sir purposely prolonged her release, bringing her close to the edge before pulling back while she concentrated on pleasuring him with her mouth.

When he slowly slipped two fingers in and started rubbing her G-spot, she knew she was done for. She could hear the smirk in his voice when he asked, "Are you ready?"

"Yes…" she murmured hungrily.

Brie grasped his shaft, taking his cock in her mouth again while he took her over the edge. The moment she started climaxing, she forced his cock deeper down her throat. Orgasming in such an intimate way was pure ecstasy for Brie.

Once her orgasm had ended, she disengaged from him and lay on the bed, panting for breath.

"I love feeling you come, babygirl," he growled huskily. Spreading her legs wider, Sir positioned himself above her.

She looked up at him hungrily, biting her lip, because her clit was delightfully sensitive. When he pressed his hard cock into her, she wrapped her legs around him and clutched his fine ass with both hands, needing to feel him deep inside her. He stroked her wet pussy, groaning in pleasure as he gave in to his own carnal desire. Together they rode the wave of their intense sensual tension as he rammed his cock into her harder.

"Come with me, téa."

Brie closed her eyes, digging her nails into his skin while he rocked her body with another orgasm. In that moment, he came inside her. A cry of sheer passion escaped her lips as she experienced his concentrated love.

After their mutual orgasms ended, he pulled her into his arms, spooning her body. Lightly kissing the back of her neck, he whispered in her ear, "Go to sleep."

Brie sighed happily, content and satisfied, and slipped easily into a peaceful slumber.

Gift of Friendship

Later that afternoon, Lea surprised Brie with a visit. She was quick to usher Lea inside, ignoring the reporters vying for their attention. Her friend was positively beaming when she waltzed into the house and seemed unfazed by the throngs of press.

"You'll never guess what Hunter has done, Stinky Cheese!"

Brie's heart instantly felt lighter just being in Lea's presence. "Tell me, girlfriend."

Lea grinned, holding her palm up. "Just give me one quick sec."

Walking to Sir's office, she knocked before peeking her head in. "Please, Sir Davis, you'll want to hear this."

Sir held Hope's hand as the little girl toddled out of the office with him. Hope was looking up at her daddy with adoration and would have crashed into the door frame if Sir hadn't acted quickly, sweeping her into his arms. Hope let out a squeal of laughter, oblivious that her daddy had just saved her from a nasty bump.

"Please sit, Sir Davis," Lea insisted, patting the couch.

He raised an eyebrow. "I trust you haven't called me out of my office to subject me to one of your jokes, Ms. Taylor."

"No, Sir Davis! Although, I do have a real doozy for you if you'd like me to share it."

"I'll pass," he answered drolly as he took a seat beside Brie and gave her a private smirk.

Brie knew Sir secretly enjoyed teasing Lea.

"Now that I've got both of your attention…" She pulled an envelope out of her large purse and handed it to Sir. "…I want to give you this, compliments of Hunter."

Sir furrowed his brow as he stared at the envelope. "What is it?"

"You have to open it to find out, Sir Davis," Lea squeaked, glancing at Brie excitedly.

Sir tore open the envelope and pulled out four tickets, fanning them out so Brie could see what they were.

Brie giggled. "Why the heck would Hunter buy us and our children tickets for a Mexican cruise?"

Lea glanced at the front door. "I bet you could use some time away from the craziness, don't you think?"

Her eyes were twinkling when she pulled a golden envelope from out of her purse. Holding it out to Brie, she gushed, "Hunter has been secretly planning this for quite a while!"

Brie took the envelope from Lea and glanced at Sir in amusement, wondering if this was some kind of elaborate joke Lea was setting up.

Her friend stared at her eagerly while Brie broke the seal and pulled out an invitation. Her eyes grew wide when she realized what she was holding. "Oh, my goodness, Lea!"

"I know! It's happening. It's really happening!" Lea squealed, jumping up and down.

Brie handed it to Sir, telling him excitedly, "We've been invited to a collaring!"

Sir immediately set Hope down and stood up, holding out his hand to Lea. "Congratulations are in order, Ms. Taylor."

Lea shook his hand enthusiastically. "I'm so happy, Sir Davis. I feel like I am about to burst into a million pieces!"

Brie jumped up off the couch and wrapped her arms around Lea. "I'm thrilled for you, girlfriend."

Lea returned her hug, nearly squeezing the breath out of her before letting go. "After Ms. Clark and then Liam, I thought I was the unluckiest girl alive and only destined for heartbreak…"

Lea's face was radiant when she declared, "But Hunter changed all that!"

Sir stared at the tickets for a moment, then tried to hand them back to her. "We can't allow you to pay for these."

Lea refused to take them back, her grin growing wider. "Hunter insists."

"Allow me to pay for the children at the very least."

"Nope! Hunter refuses to break up your sweet little family over this, and he chose this cruise line because it has a stellar children's program."

"Who else will be attending your collaring?" Brie asked her.

"Master Nosh and his wife."

Brie chuckled. "Is that all?"

Lea nodded, and explained, "Hunter and I decided to keep it private, but we both wanted to invite the two people who were instrumental in our development during our training."

Sir nodded to Lea. "I am sincerely honored, Ms. Taylor."

"So that means you'll come, Sir Davis?" she begged.

Before answering, Sir turned to Brie. "Although I think time away could prove beneficial given the circumstances, I want the final decision to be yours, babygirl."

Brie looked at Lea, overwhelmed with happiness. "I wouldn't miss it for the world, my friend!"

Lea squeaked and grabbed Brie's hands. The two of them started jumping up and down excitedly. Hope toddled over to them, bouncing on her toes in imitation.

Brie lifted her up, grinning at her. "We're going on a big boat, sweet pea!"

"I'd better get back to it, then," Sir stated. "I'm afraid I'll need to work while I'm on the ship, but I'll rearrange my schedule to make it as minimal as possible."

Lea shook her head in amazement, her eyes shining bright. "I can't believe it's really happening! Soon, I'm going to be wearing Hunter's collar."

Sir looked at Lea with pride before leaving the room, obviously happy for his former student.

Once Brie was alone with Lea, she told her, "I've never been on a cruise before."

"You're going to love it, girlfriend! My parents used to take me on one every year. They're so much fun, Stinky Cheese. There is always something to do, new places to see, and dinner is quite the adventure."

Brie smiled, liking the idea of that.

"They are going to treat you like royalty on the ship." Lea turned to Hope, saying in a sing-song voice, "I bet you are going to love it as much as I did growing up!" Tweaking her nose, she asked, "Do you know which vegetable is not allowed on a cruise, Hope?"

"Oh, no…" Brie muttered as she waited for the dreaded punchline.

Lea gleefully blurted, "Leeks!"

"Seriously, that was terrible," Brie groaned.

"I concur," Sir called out from his office.

Lea giggled and leaned down, whispering to Hope, "I've got a million more for you."

Brie gazed at Lea tenderly. Her sweet friend deserved only the best, and it thrilled Brie to no end that Hunter seemed bound and determined to give Lea exactly that.

When it was time for Lea to head out, Brie stood at the door and waved goodbye. While she watched members of the press slowly part to allow Lea's vehicle to back out of the driveway, one of the reporters shouted to her.

"Mrs. Davis, I have it on good authority that your friend Mr. Gray was involved in the murder of Greg Holloway. Can you confirm that?"

Brie quickly shut the door, her hand shaking as she turned the deadbolt.

The timing of this trip couldn't have been better, and

the reason behind it was just what her heart needed.

Brie stared up at the ship in awe after they had checked in their baggage and were walking up to the vessel. "It's so huge!"

Lea leaned in close, whispering, "That's what she said."

Giggling, Brie bumped hips with her.

Hunter told them, "This ship holds three thousand passengers, along with the crew."

With his light brown hair and pale green eyes, Hunter gave off a sexy "boy-next-door" vibe. Having a deceptively clean-cut appearance, no one would guess by looking at him that he was into serious kink. However, Hunter's commanding presence was so strong, it almost rivaled Sir's.

Looking up at the impressive ship, Hunter told Sir, "This vessel is like a small city on water."

Sir bounced Hope in his arms. "What do you think of the boat, little angel?"

Hope pointed up, babbling excitedly when someone waved at her from one of the upper decks.

Chuckling, Sir told Brie, "It seems our daughter can't wait to start her adventure."

Brie looked down at Antony cradled in her arms. He stared up at her intently, seeming to only have eyes for his mother despite the commotion all around them. That innocent gaze filled her with a sense of joyful peace.

"You're just too stinkin' cute."

Glancing at Hunter, she said, "I want to thank you again for including our children. It is especially kind when this is such a momentous occasion for the two of you."

Hunter put his arm around Lea. "After everything you have been through, Lea and I wouldn't dream of separating your family even for a short time."

Brie was overwhelmed with gratitude. "To be invited to share in this special moment means the world to me."

Lea took Brie's hand, squeezing it tight. "You know I love ya."

As they were walking up the gangway, Lea leaned in and whispered, "I remember once, there was this first-time cruiser who asked the captain, 'Do ships like these sink very often?'" She grinned at Brie. "Do you know what he said to her?"

Sensing a joke was imminent, Brie teased her by answering, "Not really."

Lea giggled, knowing Brie would not be able to resist.

"Fine! Tell me what the captain said already."

"I'll never forget it, Stinky Cheese. He said it in such a serious tone."

Brie rolled her eyes, knowing Lea was milking this one for all she was worth. "And his answer was…?"

"The captain told her with a straight face, 'Usually only once.'"

Snorting, Brie covered her mouth. She looked down at Antony and shook her head. "I can't believe your Aunt Lea would joke about something like that when we are about to board a ship."

Turning to Lea, Brie said accusingly, "You know…you're almost as bad as Rytsar. He joked with Sir about planes crashing when we were taking off from LAX."

"Okay, that *is* over the top," Lea insisted. "But my joke is funny, right?"

Brie held up her thumb and pointer finger very close together.

Sir asked with a relaxed smile. "What are you two going on about?"

"Lea just tried a new joke on me."

"Ah…" he smirked. "My condolences, babygirl."

Brie burst into giggles, but they quickly died out and she stopped dead in her tracks. Gazing upward, her jaw dropped in awe as she looked at the grand foyer of the ship. It was several stories high and looked like a setting from a fairytale castle. She loved the intricately inlaid marble flooring and the impressive staircase highlighted with golden accents and romantic lighting.

"Pretty!" Hope cried, clapping her hands together excitedly.

"It sure is pretty…" Brie murmured breathlessly.

"The dining room is just as spectacular," Lea told her with a happy sigh. "I've been wanting to take a voyage on this boat ever since it launched."

She looked at Hunter adoringly. "I never dreamed it would be for my collaring."

Hunter lifted her hand and kissed it. "Such an important moment in our lives deserves the appropriate backdrop."

She giggled. "You shouldn't spoil me so…"

He raised an eyebrow. "As your Master, I can and *will* spoil you as much as I want." With that, he grabbed the back of her neck, giving her a deep and possessive kiss.

Their chemistry was so intense that a woman walking past smiled and turned to her husband. "Must be newlyweds."

After Hunter pulled away from the kiss, he winked at Lea. Placing his hand on the small of her back, he headed toward the elevators.

Lea looked back at Brie with a blush on her cheeks. "The size of the cabins are going to surprise you."

Brie chuckled knowingly. "I already googled it, girl-friend. I know exactly what to expect—cramped quarters, no storage, a tiny bathroom, and a small porthole. But it'll be more than worth it to spend five days cruising on the ocean with you."

Lea laughed. "Of course you googled it!"

Hunter

When the doors of the elevator opened on their floor, Brie was surprised to find a man waiting in the corridor for their arrival. As soon as Hunter walked out, the well-dressed gentleman bowed his head in respect. "Welcome, Mr. Castillo."

Holding his hand out to Hunter, the man introduced himself. "My name is Remington. I'm at your disposal and happy to assist in any capacity you require."

It wasn't until that moment that Brie realized she had never heard Hunter's last name before. She hid a be-mused smile, realizing she knew very little about the man other than how much Lea loved him, and how patient and kind he'd been to Mary while she was staying at Lea's apartment.

"I trust the room is ready?" Hunter asked the man.

Remington smiled. "Of course, sir. To your exact specifications."

He then turned to address all of them. "I will be your personal butler for the voyage. If you have any questions or needs, no matter how small, please let me know."

Brie looked at Lea and raised her eyebrows. Her friend hadn't been kidding when she said they would be treated like royalty on the ship.

"Now, if you'll follow me," Remington said, "I'll escort you to your rooms."

Impressed, Brie followed behind the man as he led them down the hallway. Lea leaned in and whispered to her, "Wow, Hunter really went all out."

Remington stopped and gestured to a door on the right. "This is your stateroom, Mr. and Mrs. Davis."

Using his key card, Sir unlocked the door and opened it for Brie as Remington continued down the hallway with Lea and Hunter.

The moment Brie entered the cabin, she burst out laughing. "This is so not what I was expecting…"

Sir let out a whistle as he took in the view. "Nor I, babygirl."

Based on her research, Brie was prepared for a tiny cabin consisting of two twin beds, a small shower, and a view of the ocean through a porthole. Instead, this was a stylishly decorated suite with a queen-sized bed facing a spacious balcony overlooking the ocean. To the left was a separate room set up with two portable cribs, and on the right was a mirrored wall with a luxurious sitting area, complete with a stocked bar.

There was even a beautiful arrangement of fresh flowers on the coffee table, along with a bottle of champagne and a box of chocolates.

"This is amazing!" Brie cried as she headed to the bathroom and stopped short. Not only did the bathroom have a marble vanity and large tub, but the suite also had a walk-in closet. Shaking her head in amazement, she stepped back out, murmuring, "I can't believe this!"

"You haven't seen the balcony yet," Sir told her, opening the sliding glass door.

As she stepped out, Brie marveled at the large private deck. The balcony had an unobstructed view of the ocean because the cabin was at the back of the ship.

Not only did their balcony have chairs and a table, but there were two loungers and a hammock hanging in the corner. "We're going to have so much fun out here, Sir!"

When she turned, she noticed he was staring at the hammock. "We shall indeed, babygirl."

Brie blushed as she glanced at their two children. She was extremely grateful that Hunter had given them an extra room so they would have an opportunity to properly enjoy the hammock alone.

Heading back inside, Sir set Hope down on the sofa. He noticed she was staring longingly at the vase of flowers and pulled a stalk of pink snapdragons from it. Handing it to her, he smiled. "For you, my little angel."

Hope's eyes widened as she took the pretty snapdragons from her daddy. Grinning, Brie set Antony down on the bed, then knelt beside Hope. "Snapdragons are some of Mommy's favorite flowers. Do you know why, sweet pea?"

When Hope shook her head no, Brie put her fingertips to either side of one blossom and pressed her fingers together. It made the flower "open" its mouth.

"I love them because they can talk," Brie explained.

Using a high squeaky voice as she pressed the flower in time with her words, she said, "Hi! My name is Snappy the Dragon."

Hope giggled, then cried out, "Again!"

"What's your name, little girl?" Brie asked her, still pretending to be the flower.

Her daughter's eyes twinkled as she answered the blossom and then gave it a sweet kiss.

Brie hugged Hope. "You are too adorable!"

She was startled when someone knocked on the other side of the mirrored wall.

"Hello?" Brie called out.

She heard Lea's familiar voice. "I need you to unlock the door."

"What do you mean?"

Sir quickly scanned the wall and found a lock cleverly hidden by the design of the mirrors. When he unlocked it, the mirrored wall moved, revealing a connecting door.

"Can you believe it?" Lea squealed. "Hunter got adjoining rooms so we can hang together!"

Hunter walked in behind Lea, staring at her with pride. "Only the best for my sprite."

Lea leaned into him, murmuring, "Hunter, you've seriously thought of everything."

"This is just the beginning…" he replied with a wink.

Sir turned to Hunter. "I understand such extravagant accommodations for Ms. Taylor, but there was no need for you to splurge on us as well."

"On the contrary, Mr. Davis." He grazed Lea's cheek with his fingertips. "A person's happiness has nothing to do with their career choice or where they choose to live.

But it has everything to do with the person they choose to share life's journey with. I want these next five days to reflect the beauty of this union between Master and submissive, as well as the magnitude of what it means for both of us."

Lea purred, looking into Hunter's eyes as she nodded in agreement.

"I couldn't agree more," Sir stated, glancing at Brie. "The person you choose makes all the difference in the world."

"For that reason," Hunter continued, "I've spared no expense. I want Lea to know how much I value her as my partner, and we both want the two people responsible for this union to be present when she formally accepts my collar."

"If I'm being completely honest, I expected your family to attend," Brie told them both.

Lea chuckled. "Neither of our families understands the significance of this ceremony. They are all waiting for a wedding—which we're not opposed to. However, for Hunter and me, this collaring means more than any civil ceremony."

"Understood," Sir replied, looking tenderly at Brie.

"If there is anything I can do to make this more special for you two, I'd be more than happy to help," Brie told them both.

"Remington has everything under control," Hunter assured her.

Lea grinned at Brie. "The only thing I need from you is *you*, silly."

Her declaration touched Brie deeply. Their friendship meant the world to her. It had carried her through good times and bad. "I love you, Lea."

Grabbing Brie, Lea pressed her large boobs against her. "And I love you, Stinky Cheese. Forever and always."

When Lea let go, Brie glanced at Hunter. She felt mortified when she confessed, "Hunter, I'm embarrassed to admit that I only just learned your surname and have no idea what your first name is."

Hunter gave her a half-grin. "Well, that's easily remedied." Holding out his hand, he stated in a formal voice, "My given name is Ian."

Brie shook his hand, saying formally, "Thank you for these lovely quarters, Ian Castillo."

"Castillo…are you of Spanish descent?" Sir asked.

"I am. My father is Spanish, but I grew up in Portugal, where my mother was born."

"I visited Portugal on several occasions with my father when I was a boy," Sir told him. "It's a beautiful country rich with culture."

"*Sim*," he stated, his eyes glowing with pride.

Lea whispered to Brie. "That means 'yes' in Portuguese."

Brie turned to her and asked in surprise, "You're learning to speak Portuguese?"

Lea laughed. "Let's just say I'm trying to."

Brie hadn't noticed that Hope had climbed down from the chair and toddled her way over to Hunter. There was no mistaking how captivated she was by the young Dom when she held up the snapdragons to him.

"I think someone is smitten with you," Brie told him.

He chuckled good-naturedly and winked at Hope as he took the flowers from her. Breaking the stalk, he tucked one piece into Hope's hair and the other into Lea's.

Brie found it charming that Hunter was so easy around children despite not having any of his own and commented, "You're a real natural with kids."

He shrugged. "I was the youngest in my family and my older sisters had children while I was growing up. Having a house full of kids seems normal to me."

Brie loved getting more insight into Hunter's childhood and smiled at Lea.

Although her BFF referred to children as "little aliens", Brie felt certain Lea would make a wonderful mother based on her interactions with Brie's children.

"When do you expect Master Nosh and his wife to arrive?" Brie asked Lea.

Hunter answered for her. "They are private people and requested a quiet room far from the activities on the ship."

Sir chuckled. "I'm certain this cruise is a bit out of their comfort zone."

"It is," Hunter agreed. "However, both Nenove and Master Nosh are adventurous spirits and said they were looking forward to the experience."

Brie was excited to finally meet Nosh's wife in person. Whenever Sir spoke about her it was always with reverence. However, Nenove had never attended a gathering while Brie had been at the Training Center, so she knew very little about the woman.

Leaning over to Lea, she whispered, "Have you met

her before?"

She shook her head. "Nope. That's one reason I was so thrilled that they both agreed to come."

"This should be interesting…" Brie murmured, imagining a woman as serious and quiet as Master Nosh.

Hunter glanced at his watch. "The ship will be departing soon."

Lea grinned down at Hope. "Would you like to wave goodbye to people?"

Knowing how much her daughter loved to wave, Brie was not surprised when she nodded enthusiastically.

"It was one of my favorite things to do as a kid," Lea told Brie.

Hunter let Lea take the lead as she took them on a quick tour of the ship as they made their way to the Lido Deck. Brie was amazed by the size of the posh theater, the opulence of the formal dining room, and the engaging children's area with its kid-sized furniture, tons of toys, and an extensive craft center.

It was truly a kid's paradise.

The moment Hope saw it, she immediately tried to wiggle out of Sir's arms so she could go play.

"Don't you want to wave bye-bye, little angel?" Sir reminded her. Hope looked up at him and immediately stopped fussing. But, as he led her away, she glanced back and pointed at it longingly.

When they finally arrived at the Lido Deck, Brie was taken aback by the bird's eye view they had of the port. "I can't believe how high up we are!"

Sir lifted Hope higher to see and she started waving the second she spotted the people down below making last minute preparations for the ship's departure. One of the workers happened to look up and waved back at her, causing Hope to squeal in delight.

When the ship finally began to move, a horn blasted, announcing in a whimsical tune that the ship was leaving the port. Hope laughed as she waved enthusiastically with both hands at everyone below.

Brie was moved by her daughter's infectious joy and kissed the top of Antony's head.

Out of nowhere, an icy chill coursed through her body, leaving Brie breathless. She immediately closed her eyes, repeating to herself, *Holloway is gone. There is nothing to fear.*

"Are you okay?" Sir asked, putting his arm around her.

Brie opened her eyes and smiled, knowing her fear was unfounded. The memories of a dead man could not have power over her life anymore.

"I am, Sir," she answered with confidence.

Turning to Lea and Hunter, Brie declared, "There is no other place I would rather be than to be right here, right now."

Adventures in Dining

B rie took extra care in dressing both children for dinner. Lea insisted that kids were welcome at the formal affair and that Nenove was looking forward to meeting them.

While tying the bow on Hope's dress, Brie confessed to Sir, "I'm a tad nervous about dining with the Noshes."

He chuckled as he buttoned the cuffs of his dress shirt. "Why is that, babygirl?"

"The entire time I've been at the Training Center, I've never met Nenove and I would really hate to make a bad impression now."

"There is no chance of that." Sir cupped her chin and looked into her eyes. "They are down-to-earth people. There is no reason for you to worry."

After she finished dressing the children, Sir helped Brie into her gown and zipped up the back, kissing her bare shoulder when he was done.

Glancing in the mirror again, he adjusted his tie. "I,

for one, am excited about tonight. An evening spent with the Noshes is a true gift."

"Do you miss working with him?"

"I do," he admitted. "Nosh keeps an intense schedule. Working with him proved to be the only opportunity I had of us running into each other."

Brie frowned. "I'm sorry to hear that, Sir. I know how much you look up to him, not only as a Dominant, but as a mentor."

Nodding, he told her, "He was instrumental in inspiring me to become the man I am today." Looking at Brie, he stated matter-of-factly, "I would not have been worthy of collaring you as my submissive without his instruction."

She smiled. "I'm sure that's not true."

Wrapping his arms around her, Sir replied, "Trust me, babygirl. His guidance helped me remain steadfast in my values and vision as a Dominant for all these years. It's the reason I am confident in Lea's choice of a partner. Master Nosh would not hold Hunter in high regard if he had not earned it."

Brie's smile grew wider. Hugging him back, she said, "I'm thrilled for Lea. I'll never forget the joy I felt when you placed this collar around my neck." She touched the dangling pearl lightly. "It changed my life."

"Mine as well," Sir agreed, tracing the metal collar with a finger. "It took great courage to offer your submission to me."

"It took even greater courage for you to leave the Training Center behind."

He leaned down to kiss her. "Best decision I ever made…"

Brie lingered behind, holding Hope's hand as they walked into the dining room. She watched from afar as Hunter formally introduced Lea to Nosh's wife. The woman had long, dark hair which was bound into a ponytail. She flashed a warm smile at Lea, and Brie was surprised to see her give Lea a big hug.

This was not the reserved woman Brie was expecting.

Once Lea and Hunter were seated, Sir guided Brie to the table while cradling Antony in one arm.

"Nenove, I am honored to introduce you to Brianna."

The woman nodded to Sir respectfully before opening her arms wide to Brie. "What a pleasure to meet Sir Davis's submissive! This moment has been a long time coming."

"It has," Brie agreed, returning the woman's welcoming hug.

"Did you know I had a vision of you the night Sir Davis graduated from his training with my husband?"

Brie crinkled her brow and looked at Sir in surprise. "I did not know that."

Sir snorted. "This is news to me, Nenove."

Smiling at Sir, she explained, "I only told Ese'he about it."

"I remember…" Master Nosh stated with a slight smile on his lips.

"And yet, you never told me," Sir remarked, raising

an eyebrow at Master Nosh.

He replied in a solemn tone, "Had you known the future, you may have strayed from your chosen path."

"While that is possible…" Sir paused, glancing at Brie for a moment, "…I would not have believed you."

"Because you would have deemed yourself unworthy of her," Master Nosh asserted.

"Exactly. In fact, I felt that way the day I collared her."

Brie was surprised when the head trainer's low chuckle filled the air. "Then it is good I kept Nenove's vision from you."

"But it is good to see it fulfilled!" Nosh's wife exclaimed, her brown eyes sparkling as she looked at Antony. "You have a fine, healthy son." She then turned to Hope and knelt beside her. "And a strong daughter to be proud of."

"Her name is Hope," Brie informed her.

Nenove glanced up, looking pleased. "That is a powerful name."

Smiling, she looked at their little girl and said, "Hope. The strong warrior with a gentle heart."

Hope grinned, throwing her small arms around Nenove's neck. The instant bond they seemed to share was heartwarming to Brie.

Standing up, Nenove then glanced at Antony and told Sir, "Your son is much like you."

"I certainly hope not," Sir muttered under his breath.

Brie brushed her son's cheek lovingly. "Well, I do. Because he's perfect like his daddy."

Sir smirked, saying nothing as two servers came up

to the table, one carrying a booster for Hope and a highchair.

While they seated the children, the host escorted a stylish woman to the table to join them. Judging by her elegant clothes and her understated confidence, Brie was certain the woman must be a model.

"Good evening. My name is Ivetta. It's a pleasure to meet all of you."

Lea, who was seated beside her, shook her hand warmly. "I have to confess that this is my favorite part about dinner. I love getting to meet new people. I'm Lea, and this is my boyfriend, Hunter."

"Lovely to meet you both," Ivetta replied, shaking their hands.

Lea then took the lead and formally introduced everyone to the new guest, explaining to her, "They are all friends of ours."

Ivetta held out her hand to shake each of their hands, commenting, "Isn't it wonderful to spend a cruise with your friends?"

"Have you come with anyone?" Brie asked her.

"Yes. Unfortunately, my friend couldn't join me for dinner tonight. She spent too much time on the Lido Deck this afternoon and has a nice sunburn to show for it."

"Oh no! That's not a fun way to start the cruise," Brie cried, feeling sympathy for the girl.

"Don't worry, Nora is covered in aloe vera at this very moment and ordering in tonight. She claims she's happy about it because she'll have a nice tan by the time we reach Cabo San Lucas."

While everyone at the table was laughing, the host escorted an elderly man to their table, filling the last seat.

"James, how lovely it is to see you again," Ivetta gushed. "How long has it been?"

He took her hand and kissed it courteously. "Far too long, Ivetta."

"It certainly has," she agreed, smiling as they both sat down.

"How has Canada been treating you?" he asked her.

"It's been frightfully cold," she said, laughing. "Which is the whole reason I'm here."

James grinned. "You need to move to Texas like Besse kept telling you to."

Giggling, she answered, "I know, I know…"

"How do you two know each other?" Brie asked with interest.

James answered with fondness, "My wife and I were seasoned travelers and we'd had the pleasure of Ivetta's company on numerous occasions."

Brie picked up on the fact he said "were" and wondered what had happened to his wife but she felt uncomfortable asking.

After Lea finished introducing James to everyone, he immediately said, "So, I just gotta ask. How did the six of you meet? You seem like a mighty diverse group."

Brie saw the twinkle in Lea's eyes when she answered, "Well, I had an interest in higher education and took a course where I ended up meeting Brie. We became best friends and she fell in love with Mr. Davis, who was once a student of Mr. Nosh, who also instructed my boyfriend, Hunter, years later."

James leaned in, asking Lea, "What did you get your degree in, Ms. Taylor?"

Lea, as cool as a cucumber, was quick to answer, "Inter*disciplinary* studies." She made sure to emphasize "disciplinary" when she said it. "One thing led to another, and here we all are together on this ship."

"Well, ain't that somethin'!" James exclaimed, sitting back in his chair. He looked at the six of them in amazement.

Brie fought hard not to burst out laughing and was saved when their server came to the table with chilled dishes containing pats of butter in the shape of flowers and baskets of fresh rolls.

While Brie broke off small pieces of the roll and fed them to Hope, the others at the table started sharing what they did for a living. While Brie listened, she suddenly understood why Lea had said dinners on the ship were such an adventure. Due to the unique setting and the diversity of the travelers gathered at each table, people seemed to be more open and asked questions of each other.

"May I ask what you do for a living, Mrs. Nosh?" Ivetta asked Nenove.

Through Ivetta's simple question, Brie learned that Nenove oversaw several important programs for the Cheyenne people. She was part of a council that aided impoverished families struggling to care for their children. But, in doing so, she'd become acutely aware of the needs of their Elders. She now spearheaded a program to not only ensure their health and wellbeing but to actively help the Elders to carry on their traditions and teach them to the younger generations.

"I am driven to work hard every day, and must often travel back to the reservation." Nenove informed Ivetta, "There are only eleven thousand of us left. We cannot ignore the needs of our youth, and we *must* not lose the wisdom of our Elders."

Her mission reminded Brie of Tatianna's passion for the native languages of Russia.

Master Nosh stated with pride. "Nenove is a warrior in her own right. She is living proof that a steadfast vision can change a nation."

Nenove placed her hand on his and looked at him with equal admiration. "I am grateful to be partnered with a great man who shares the same vision and is willing to make sacrifices for his people."

All this time, Brie had assumed Nenove's absence at the Training Center was due to her being too reserved and private, but the opposite was actually true. She was a warm person involved in important humanitarian efforts.

Brie admired Nenove—and Master Nosh as well! He fully supported his wife's work and accepted the sacrifices that work entailed. They were both extraordinary people in their own right but, together, they were truly a magnificent force in the world.

After enjoying a dinner of cocktail shrimp, chicken cordon bleu, and deliciously seasoned new potatoes, in the company of such a fine group of people, Brie was feeling good. The conversation remained lively throughout the dinner, giving Lea the opportunity to throw in a couple of her jokes, while Nenove kept Hope entertained by teaching her simple words in Cheyenne.

But the evening wasn't over.

Dessert was a decadent cake layered with chocolate mousse and covered in a rich ganache. Sir picked up his fork and cut a slice of Brie's cake, slowly bringing it to her lips. Whispering in her ear, he told her, "After I feed you this bite, I want you to get up and go to the restroom. Take off your panties and hand them to me once you return."

Brie's eyes widened when she heard his command. With a racing heart, she opened her mouth and took the bite he offered.

Chewing it slowly, she felt sensual tingles coursing through her and was eager to complete his sexy task.

After swallowing the delicious morsel, she politely excused herself from the table and went to the bathroom. Once inside the stylish restroom, she slipped off her lace panties and stuffed them in her purse. Heading back out, she walked through the large dining area full of people with her chest out and her head held high but at a respectful angle.

Although this was a simple task, it really turned Brie on and caused her erect nipples to rub the material of her lace bra. The sensation felt deliciously wicked.

Brie sat back down next to Sir and held her purse under the table. While he continued his conversation with James, she pulled out her panties and wadded them into a ball.

Nonchalantly handing them to her Master under the table, she felt a jolt of electricity when their hands touched and he took them from her. Brie pretended to listen intently to the conversation, but she was far too distracted to think.

"Aren't you going to eat your cake?" Lea asked her. "It's incredible!"

Brie smiled, blushing slightly. "I'm suddenly not all that hungry."

Lea raised her eyebrows, looked at Sir, and gave her a knowing smirk. Hunter noticed her smirk and glanced at Brie, as did Master Nosh.

Brie's blush grew deeper. She was certain the three of them now recognized that a kinky power exchange was happening at the table.

Sir made no indication he was aware, continuing the discussion with James and inviting Ivetta to join in. He then glanced at his watch and turned to Brie. "It's getting close to the children's bedtime. We better go before the two begin to fuss."

Brie smiled inwardly when she answered, "I agree."

However, Nenove was reluctant to part with Hope, telling Brie, "Your daughter picks up our language unusually fast."

Glancing at Sir, Brie laughed. "Then Hope takes after her daddy in that regard."

Hope waved at Nenove and said goodbye when Brie picked her up. Nenove waved at her, mentioning to Brie, "The Cheyenne do not have a word for goodbye. We expect to see each other again, so there was never a need for the word."

"I love that," Brie declared.

Nenove nodded, her eyes twinkling as she looked at Hope.

"This is not goodbye," Brie told the group as the four of them readied to leave. "This is just 'until we see you again.'"

James grinned. "My wife, Besse, used to say that exact same thing! The fact is, when you're on a cruise, you are pretty much guaranteed to see each other again during the trip. And, if you're lucky," he said, looking at Ivetta with fondness, "you'll get to see them year after year."

Ivetta smiled. "I sure miss Besse, but I know she's here in spirit."

"That she is!" he agreed wholeheartedly.

Brie looked at James with new understanding, sad to learn that his wife was dead.

"No need to feel bad," James told her as if picking up on her sadness. "My Besse is always with me, and I can tell she's smiling down on us right now."

After getting Sir's nonverbal permission, Brie gave James a hug before they left the table, feeling deeply touched by the love the man had for his late wife.

Good Girl

B rie was acutely aware of Sir's presence as they walked back to their cabin.

Once inside, they performed their parental tasks with Sir reading a book to the children while Brie undressed them and put their pajamas on. Tucking them in, Brie kissed both of their foreheads and whispered to each of them, "I'm so proud of you."

She then left the room with Sir, after he turned out the light and shut the connecting door. Brie trembled in submissive excitement when he pulled her panties from his pocket and gave her a sexy smile.

"Go out to the balcony and stare out at the ocean while you wait for me. I will stay behind to make sure the children are fast asleep."

Brie bowed her head, purring, "It would be my greatest pleasure, Sir."

Opening the sliding glass door, Brie walked out to see the sky lit up with stars and a sliver of a crescent moon overhead.

"Wow…" she murmured, mesmerized by how bright the stars were. She could easily see the impressive swath of the Milky Way across the sky.

The vastness of space was truly awe-inspiring.

She could hear Sir moving inside the cabin and smiled to herself. Leaning harder against the railing, she spread her legs so she could feel the light ocean breeze swirl up her dress, lightly teasing her bare pussy. Brie was already wet and eagerly anticipating Sir's next command.

Goosebumps of excitement rose on her skin when she heard his footsteps approaching her on the balcony.

"Enjoying the view, babygirl? I know I am…"

She smiled as she looked back to find him holding out a martini to her.

"The sky is incredible tonight, Sir," she replied. "But not as incredible as you."

He chuckled. "Being compared to the universe is a bit of a stretch."

"I can only look at and admire the stars from afar, but you…I can touch…and taste."

Sir's eyes flashed with desire, but he remained cool and composed as he handed her the glass and lifted his. "First, we drink."

Brie took a sip of the martini and sighed happily. She swore Sir was as skilled at making martinis as he was at being a Dom. He intuitively knew how to combine the simple ingredients to make her tongue and body purr with happiness.

Walking up beside her, Sir joined Brie to look out at the ocean while the two of them sipped their drinks in silence. She was intoxicated by his commanding presence as she admired the dark sky lit up with tiny diamonds. It seemed incredible to be here, in the middle of the ocean, on a beautiful night like this.

Sir took his time to enjoy the drink and Brie followed suit, taking small sips. She appreciated how her Master could take a moment like this and draw it out so beautifully.

A gust of wind suddenly swirled up her legs and she bit her lip, enjoying the flirtatious breeze that teased her and the warmth of the alcohol.

When they were both finished with their martinis, Sir took her glass and placed both of them on the table nearby.

He then commanded, "Stare straight ahead and stay still, téa."

Brie sucked in a sharp breath, excited that the scene had officially begun.

Sir walked up behind her and ran his fingers lightly down her arm. "I consider myself fortunate that a woman as beautiful as you would come to my suite."

She smiled inwardly, realizing he was setting up a role-playing scenario. When she opened her mouth to reply, he told her, "No words tonight. You must remain silent. No one else can know you are here. Do you understand?"

Brie nodded slightly in response.

"Good," he stated with a low growl.

Moving her hair to one side, he leaned down and lightly blew on her neck, sending a cascade of sensual chills coursing through her body.

Such a simple act had her pussy gushing with need.

She then felt his warm lips on her skin and let out a soft gasp, her nipples tightening into hard buds.

Sir trailed his kisses from her neck to her shoulder, then lifted her arm and continued his way down her arm until he reached her hand. Once there, he turned it palm-side up, and kissed it lightly before letting her go.

Brie let her arm slowly fall to her side and waited breathlessly.

Putting his arms on the rail to either side of her, he pressed his body against her. She felt the pressure of his rigid cock.

"Do you feel my desire for you?"

She nodded.

"I ache to possess you," he said gruffly.

In her head, Brie was begging him to claim her but, outwardly, she remained silent and still.

The occasional cheers and laughter of people having fun on the upper decks broke the heated silence between them and added to the scene.

Sir grabbed her waist and slowly inched the material of her skirt up with his fingers, inch by sexy inch. She was trembling in anticipation when the hem of her skirt finally crested the swell of her ass, exposing her to him.

"Perfection," he murmured huskily.

Holding the dress up with one hand, he caressed her ass with the other, causing a new set of goosebumps to rise up on her skin.

"Are you wet?" he asked as he slipped his fingers between her legs.

Brie held back a moan when she felt his fingers glide over her wet pussy.

"You're dripping for me, aren't you?"

She nodded again, drawn into his erotic scene.

Brie gasped softly when he pressed his finger into her.

"Shh…"

She immediately pressed her lips together.

Sir pulled his finger out and leaned forward so she could watch as he brought his finger to his lips and sucked her wetness from it. He straightened again, and the butterflies started when she heard him unbuckle his belt and unzip his pants.

"I need to know if you feel as good as you taste."

Brie bit her bottom lip when the head of his cock rubbed against her pussy in the moments before he pushed himself inside.

"Fuck…" Sir groaned as he gave her a hard thrust.

Her body eagerly responded to his forceful penetration, demanding more.

"Hands back," he ordered.

Brie immediately put her hands behind her back, and he tightly wrapped his hand around both of her wrists and bent her forward so he had full access to her pussy.

"Remember, not a sound," he reminded her as he pushed her dress up higher and out of the way.

With her arms bound by Sir's hand and his cock deep inside her, Brie was lost in a heavenly bliss. Grasping her waist with his free hand, he started to pound her, his strokes long and deep. She panted heavily, welcoming every hard thrust of his cock. He had managed to get her so wet that the slippery sound of their union filled the air.

Then he changed it up…

"That ass is so fine."

Brie trembled in anticipation when he let go of her wrists and commanded in a low voice, "Hands on the rail. Press your body against the railing."

Brie grasped the rail with both hands and leaned her torso against it. He hiked her dress even higher and stood back for a moment to admire her.

"Your ass is the finest I've ever seen," he stated in a tone of reverence. Running his hands over her skin, he caressed her buttocks before lightly spanking them.

Leaning in close, he told her, "I want to feel the tight constriction of your ass around my cock as I come inside it."

Brie let out a tiny gasp, desperate for that connection.

"You want me to fuck your ass, don't you?" he murmured knowingly.

She immediately nodded, giddy at the thought.

There was no need for extra lube tonight because she had made enough natural lube of her own. Sir rubbed his cock against her pussy, coating it in her abundant excitement. He then pulled back and grasped his cock, slowly pressing the head of it against her anus.

Brie closed her eyes, longing to feel the challenge of his shaft.

"Give yourself to me…" he whispered hoarsely.

She held her breath as he began with gentle thrusts, slowly forcing her body to open to him. She could not hold back her gasp when the head of his cock suddenly slipped inside.

He slapped her right buttock in response, but continued his lustful invasion, telling her, "Good girls orgasm when their ass is filled with come."

Brie heard someone open the door of the balcony beside theirs, and soon the rich smell of a cigar reached her nostrils. Whoever it was, there was no doubt they were going to be there for a long time, enjoying a smoke.

Sir grasped her hips tightly with both hands. Undeterred, he began stroking her ass, forcing himself deeper inside her. He made no sound as he claimed her anally under the stars while the stranger on the other side of the divider puffed leisurely on their cigar.

Inspired by their unexpected audience, Sir put his hands on either side of hers, grasping the railing for leverage. Brie looked back at him hungrily, inviting him to fuck her even harder.

Embracing the demands of his cock, Brie forced her body to relax, reveling in his challenging strokes. She felt empowered as he gave in to his carnal need, and the pure joy of it overwhelmed her senses.

Sir reached down with one hand and began playing with her clit. The combination of his cock dominating her ass while he teased her pussy drove her wild. She longed to cry out, expressing her pleasure, but she remained silent as she received his focused attention.

Suddenly, Sir stopped and forced his shaft even deeper. She could feel the pulses of his cock as the warmth of his seed filled her ass when he came.

Brie struggled to stay quiet when his fingers returned to her clit with his cock still wedged deep inside her, while he slowly drew out a powerful, shuddering orgasm from her.

The faint smell of the stranger's cigar lingered in the air as Brie's hips bucked against Sir of their own accord. Brie lost herself in the moment as she rode the intense wave of pleasure he'd created.

After the last pulse ended, Sir leaned down and whispered in her ear. "Good girl."

Pulling out slowly, he turned her around and gave Brie a passionate kiss, expressing his deep love for her. She melted into his powerful embrace and returned his ardent kisses with equal fervor.

Their sexy scene had turned Brie on, leaving her captivated by the abundance of love Sir had lavished on her. When he took her hand, she felt like she was walking on clouds as she blissfully followed him back inside the cabin.

Sir headed to the bathroom, where he first shed his clothes and then took hers before turning on the shower. With gentle hands, he lathered her skin and kissed her repeatedly as they stood together under the warm cascade of water. It felt deliciously decadent and incredibly sweet.

Afterward, Sir wrapped her in a large towel and kissed her again.

Tears filled Brie's eyes when she looked up at him. "Thank you for tonight. This is the first time since…" Her voice trailed off for a moment as she attempted to find the right words. "Tonight, I felt fully free from any barriers of the past."

Looking deep into her eyes, he stated, "That was my hope and intention."

Overflowing with gratitude, she told him, "You are truly amazing, Master."

"You inspire me, téa."

With This Collar

B rie spent the day at the spa with Lea on the same day the ship was expected to arrive at the port in Cabo San Lucas.

Wanting to make sure Lea was thoroughly pampered, Hunter had booked a full day. The two of them started the morning with a full body massage, a luxurious facial, and a mani-pedi combination.

Lea then received a body waxing and ended her spa experience in the salon, where the experienced stylists took charge of her hair and makeup.

Naturally, Lea kept her stylists in stitches with her corny jokes. "I went to get a massage, and the masseuse told me he was going to work out all of my kinks. So, you know what I did?"

"What?" the hairstylist asked gleefully.

"I flew out of that place faster than a toupee in a hurricane!"

The other clients in the salon joined in the laughter.

"Talking about flying, time's almost up. Ready for

your big reveal?"

Lea nodded eagerly. The stylist turned Lea around in the chair to face the mirror—and the room fell silent. The stylists had chosen to enhance her natural beauty rather than hide it under heavy makeup. And her short hair was light and feathery, reminding Brie of a cute little pixie.

But what really struck Brie was Lea's inner glow. She had never seen her girlfriend look this happy before in all the years she'd known her.

"Oh, Lea…" Brie said breathlessly. "You look absolutely stunning!"

Lea clapped her hands excitedly, showing off her beautifully manicured nails, while the other women showered her with compliments.

Brie grinned. "Hunter isn't going to be able to take his eyes off of you, girlfriend."

Lea jumped out of the salon chair and crushed Brie in a big hug. "I feel higher than the best sub high right now!"

Brie laughed as she returned Lea's heartfelt hug and whispered, "Just wait until he places the collar around your neck."

As the two of them were leaving the salon together, Brie asked her, "So, have you seen the collar yet?"

Lea's eyes twinkled. "Nope, Hunter insisted on surprising me."

Brie bumped hips with her as they walked. "Well, that should be a fun surprise."

"I know!" she squeaked.

Hunter had rented a yacht for the special event, as well as hired a professional photographer to capture the ceremony. Brie boarded the vessel with Sir and was blown away when she saw the couple.

The two looked like royalty.

Lea's gown had a silver corset-style top that accentuated her voluptuous breasts and a full princess skirt of silver that transitioned into a beautiful pink ombre at the bottom. Hunter wore a formal gray suit with a light pink tie that matched the color scheme of Lea's dress.

He walked up to greet them, explaining, "We're heading out to the natural arch called Land's End to perform the ceremony."

Master Nosh nodded thoughtfully beside them. "For an occasion as sacred as this, you have picked a fine setting."

"I agree with Ese'he," Nenove said, bowing her head to Hunter. "What an unexpected treat that we get to see the arch up close while the two of you exchange vows."

Hunter looked at Lea and smiled. "I want our beginning to reflect the immensity of my feelings for her."

Brie was touched by how Hunter had put great thought into every detail of the collaring ceremony. It was as grand as an elaborate wedding and, by his own declaration, just as important.

While the photographer set up her equipment, the captain of the yacht slowly guided the vessel to the famous rock formation.

"How are you feeling, Lea?" Brie asked while Hope pointed excitedly at Lea's pretty dress.

"I feel like a princess," she grinned, doing a twirl for Hope.

Hunter overheard Lea and leaned in, telling her in a hushed voice, "I'm glad to hear it, sprite. Doing BDSM scenes while dressed as a knight is my favorite kind of kink." He nodded to the photographer who was motioning to him. Looking back at Lea, he added with a wink, "You might say it's a kink in my armor."

Lea's eyes lit up in surprise when he walked away. "That has got to be the cutest joke I've ever heard in my life…"

"This is definitely a match made in heaven." Brie giggled, feeling giddy for her friend.

As the boat neared the arch, the vessel slowed down, and Brie held Hope up to look over the railing at all the colorful fish swimming in the clear blue water below.

"This is such an incredible place to hold a collaring ceremony," Brie told Sir.

"Are you jealous?" he asked.

Brie turned to him and smiled. "Not even a tiny bit. I wouldn't change a thing about our collaring ceremony, even though you crushed my heart."

Sir chuckled lightly, wrapping an arm around her. "It was an unfortunate necessity, babygirl. The established rules of the school required it, and I needed a moment to decide how I would proceed after I watched you walk away from me."

Brie stood on tiptoes to kiss him. "Even though I never meant for you to step down as Headmaster, I'm grateful for the decision you made." She glanced at Antony and Hope, adding, "We all are."

Sir took her hand and kissed it gently. "I can't imagine my life without you or the children in it."

As the boat slowly pulled up to the rock formation, Master Nosh, Hunter and Lea took their places at the bow of the ship. Nenove stood beside Hunter, her head lowered, while Sir and Brie stood beside Lea.

Hunter had requested that Master Nosh officiate the collaring ceremony. A man of few words, the head trainer kept it simple and succinct.

"Ian Castillo and Lea Taylor have asked us here to stand witness today. Nothing in this life is as important as the partner you choose to walk life's journey with."

Turning to Hunter first, he asked, "Hunter, are you secure in your decision to be her Master?"

He gazed at Lea and said confidently, "I am."

Master Nosh then turned to Lea. "Sprite, are you secure in your decision to be his submissive?"

She gave Hunter an adoring smile. "I am, Master Nosh."

"Because Hunter and sprite are both graduates of the Training Center, they have chosen to follow the official collaring ceremony of the school. However, they will finish it with words they have composed for one another."

Sir handed Hunter a square velvet box. Taking it from him, Hunter turned to Lea. With a glint in his eye, he commanded, "Open the box, sprite."

Her hands were trembling when Lea opened the hinged box. She let out a pleased gasp. "It's beautiful…"

When Lea picked up the collar to admire it, Brie could see that the thin gold band was etched with two intertwined vines that reached around the entire length of the collar. Set in the center of the gold band was a stunning pink jewel in the shape of a heart and the back had a delicate golden lock.

Hunter told Lea, "The vines represent the two of us, and the heart represents the love that binds us."

She looked up at him with tears in her eyes. "Oh, Hunter…the meaning behind it is as beautiful as the collar itself."

He nodded, looking pleased. "Take the key as well, sprite."

Lea picked up the golden key on a chain from the velvet box. Brie noticed that the key was etched with the same vine pattern as the collar.

Shutting the box, Hunter handed it back to Sir.

Master Nosh then commanded in an official tone, "Ms. Taylor, present your collar."

Lea gracefully knelt before Hunter and bowed her head while she held up the collar and key to him.

Hunter looked down at her proudly as he took both the collar and the key. "I accept this collar as a symbol of the offering of yourself to me and promise to thoughtfully guide and lead you."

Brie felt butterflies, recalling the joy and relief that flooded through her when Sir had said those exact words.

A chime rang through the salty ocean air, marking the beginning of the formal ceremony. Glancing back, Brie saw it was the captain who had rung it.

Hunter went down on one knee. "You belong to me from this day onward. I will do all within my power to protect and keep you as you join me on this journey."

Brie trembled as she watched Hunter fasten the collar around Lea's neck and then clicked the lock into place.

Grazing her fingers over her own collar, Brie appreciated the weight of it around her throat because of the way it acted as a constant and beloved reminder of their dynamic.

Standing up, Hunter gazed down at Lea possessively. "You will wear this symbol of my ownership as a sign of our commitment to one another."

With her head still lowered, Lea vowed, "I accept this symbol of your ownership and will wear it proudly for all to see, Hunter."

"And I will wear this key as a symbol of our commitment," Hunter replied in turn, taking the gold chain from her and placing the key around his neck.

In a commanding voice, he then announced for all to hear, "You now belong to me."

"I now belong to you," Lea echoed, looking up at him with devotion.

"Sprite, I accept your request to serve me and will honor your needs and desires," Hunter vowed. "Trust that I will put your best interests foremost in my dominance over you. Your happiness, health, and well-being are in my care, and I will consciously tend to them because you are a part of me."

"Hunter, I will honor and love you as I serve you to the best of my ability. My submission to you is freely given. I am now a part of you and will respect your dominance over me as our lives become one." Lea then leaned forward and kissed both of his feet as a gesture of her submission.

Master Nosh spoke again. "As Master and submissive, they will now address each other."

Gazing down at Lea, Hunter said, "I was attracted to your beauty, but I became captivated by your depth of compassion. Where others may see you as the queen of jokes, I understand the importance behind them. You seek to make the world a kinder place. I admire that, sprite. It is my honor to assist you in that endeavor, while I explore and expand our connection as your Master."

"My Master…" Lea purred, looking up into his eyes and momentarily losing herself in his gaze.

When Master Nosh cleared his throat, she giggled self-consciously.

Smiling at Hunter, she gushed, "I appreciate you called me 'the queen of jokes'."

Brie had to stifle her giggle.

Bowing her head to Hunter before she continued, Lea said, "Master, you see me in a way no other person can. I felt it the very first time we met at the Center, when I experienced your skill with the violet wand. Every day since that, I have been in awe of you. Although today makes it official, I have been your devoted submissive since that day we met. I am honored to wear your collar and I will follow you with a happy heart wherever you choose to lead me."

In a commanding voice that gave Brie happy chills,

Hunter said, "Stand before your Master."

Brie set Hope down and broke out in enthusiastic applause with everyone else, crying tears of joy for her sweet friend.

Up to that point, the photographer had been respectful about not disturbing the ceremony while she was taking pictures. Now she moved forward and directed Hunter and Lea, wanting to capture the magic of the golden hour as she photographed the happy couple with the sun setting behind them.

After Brie bowed to Master Nosh, complimenting him for his part in the ceremony, she turned to Nenove. "Wasn't it a beautiful ceremony?" Wiping away joyful tears, Brie sighed. "I couldn't be happier for them."

Looking at the couple with a twinkle in her eye, Nenove stated, "A good match between a Dominant and submissive has the power to change the world."

Glancing at Sir, Brie said, "I couldn't agree more."

Once everyone returned to the cruise ship, they attended a private reception in Hunter and Lea's cabin to celebrate their new union.

Lea's cabin was even larger and brimming with fresh-cut flowers. The room smelled heavenly.

However, it was the incredible balcony that wowed Brie. The thing was huge and had two hammocks swinging side by side, as well as its own hot tub. As the evening progressed, everyone headed out to the balcony to enjoy the dark ocean and starry sky.

Brie was admiring Lea's new collar when Hunter walked up and informed them, "The heart is a pink diamond."

Lea immediately touched the jewel set in the collar hanging from her neck. "What? Pink diamonds are a real thing?"

"You are touching one right now," he replied, chuckling. "I thought it was fitting because you are a rare find and pink becomes you."

Lea stared at him for a moment before throwing her arms around her Master, crushing him in a boob-a-licious hug.

Brie was suddenly reminded of the pink corset Lea used to wear at the Training Center and smiled to herself. She never would have guessed then that the girl with big boobs and a cheesy sense of humor would become her dearest friend.

"Did I hear you correctly? Sir asked as he walked over to join them. "That is a pink diamond?"

"It is," Hunter stated proudly, gazing at Lea's collar.

"That is a unique gem," Sir stated, admiring the sparkling jewel.

"I've been saving up for this day for quite some time," Hunter said enthusiastically.

"The fact that you laid aside money is a testament to your commitment as a Dominant," Sir stated in approval. "Recklessly spending money you don't have would show a serious lack of judgment and concern for Ms. Taylor's well-being."

"I agree, Sir Davis," Hunter replied, looking at Lea

thoughtfully. "If I couldn't keep my finances in order, I would not feel confident in taking the lead as her Master. I have found that things of great value demand personal sacrifice."

It never occurred to Brie that a person's finances could have any bearing on a Dominant's fitness to lead. Thinking back on it, she realized that every Dom she worked with at the Submissive Training Center was fiscally responsible. It had nothing to do with how much money they made—only that they were good stewards of the income they brought in. If a Dominant could not be trusted with money, Brie knew it would be difficult for a submissive to trust them in other areas as well.

Master Nosh joined the conversation. He was staring at his wife while she explained to Hope that Nenove meant "my home" and that Master Nosh's name Ese'he meant "the Sun".

"Nenove never tires of teaching," he stated with warmth in his voice.

"I admire her passion for the Cheyenne language," Brie told him.

Master Nosh nodded. It was obvious to Brie that he was extremely proud of his wife.

Turning to Lea, Master Nosh stated somberly, "I have stated on numerous occasions that Hunter is the best student I have ever trained."

Lea nodded, bowing to the head trainer respectfully.

Brie held her breath, wondering what Master Nosh would say next.

A slight smile played across the head trainer's lips when he told Lea, "I also had the privilege of working directly with you when you were part of my staff. Your impeccable training is a testament to Sir Davis, but it is your compassionate spirit and open heart that make you an exceptional submissive. I cannot think of a better pairing."

"Thank you, Master Nosh," Lea gushed, bowing low.

Brie could not imagine a higher compliment coming from the seasoned trainer.

Master Nosh held out his hand to Hunter. "May the blessing that you are to each other be an encouragement to the many who cross your path in the years to come."

Hunter shook his hand firmly. "I appreciate every lesson and correction you have given me, Master Nosh." Glancing at Lea, he added, "I plan to lead based on the firm foundation you have instilled in me."

Brie noticed that Sir was looking at Master Nosh with an expression of gratitude and veneration.

She realized that each of them was indebted to Master Nosh. Without his dedication and insight as head trainer of the Dominant course, the four of them wouldn't be here right now, and her children would not exist.

Brie fought the urge to fall to her knees and kneel before Master Nosh out of profound gratitude. Instead of bowing, she made a silent vow to find a meaningful way to honor the esteemed trainer and his submissive.

Pirates

The next morning, Brie stood on the Lido Deck by the rail with Lea and Hope and marveled at the dolphins. The playful creatures were jumping and chattering loudly as they rode the waves caused by the wake of the ship.

It was truly magical and had Hope laughing gleefully.

Brie tilted her head up and closed her eyes to bask in the warmth of the sun while the sea breeze teased her long hair. "I can't believe it's such a beautiful day."

Lea bumped shoulders with her. "Well, I can. The best kind of weather always comes with a light Brieeee-zz."

Brie shook her head in amusement. "You're such a goofball."

"I'm being serious," Lea said, grinning back at her. "Today wouldn't be as perfect if you weren't here with me."

Giving her a tight squeeze, Brie stared at her friend's shiny new collar and asked, "How does it feel to officially be Hunter's submissive?"

Caressing the gold band, Lea surprised Brie when her tone turned serious. "I didn't realize it until last night…even though Hunter and I have been together for a while and our chemistry is off the charts, but…I don't think I ever really felt safe."

Brie frowned. "What do you mean?"

"After having my heart broken by Samantha and surviving what happened with Liam and his twin brother, I didn't really trust things would work out for us—especially because it felt so wonderful. I think I've been waiting to be hurt again."

Brie looked at her with sympathy. "That's so sad, Lea."

"I had no idea how much I was holding back until last night when I was laying in Hunter's arms. Out of nowhere, I just started to bawl and couldn't get myself to stop." Looking at Brie with tearful eyes, she confessed, "He actually thought I was having second thoughts."

"Poor Hunter!" Brie exclaimed.

"You're not kidding." She groaned. "Even though I didn't have any second thoughts, it took me a while to figure out that all of those tears I was crying were tears of relief. But can you imagine? After everything he did to make the day special, there I was—crying my freaking eyes out."

"How did he handle it?"

"Of course he was distressed—naturally. But he held me close and comforted me through my tears."

Smiling confidently, Brie said, "That right there is the testament of a true Dom."

Lea smirked at her. "There was *one* good thing that came from all that crying."

"What was that?"

Lea put her hands over Hope's ears. "Hunter and I had the best fuck of our entire lives!"

Brie snorted. "Sir and I heard that part…"

"Then you know it went on for hours!" Lea grinned.

Removing her hands from Hope's ears, Lea kissed the little girl on the head. "I'm not sure if it was all of those tears or the fact that I was wearing his collar, but man… Best. Night. Ever!"

"You may think it can't be topped, but I'm speaking from experience when I say this is just the beginning for you two. It's the reason I can't stop smiling for you—" Brie's voice trailed off when she spotted Sir and Hunter, who was holding Antony.

Lea saw them too and waved frantically, pointing to the water. "You have to see this! There are dolphins jumping in the waves."

Again, Brie was impressed with the easy way Hunter had around children. But the moment Antony saw Brie, he immediately started to fuss. Taking him from Hunter, Brie pointed to the dolphins and said excitedly, "Do you see them? Look how high they can jump."

While Brie was watching the dolphins, she noticed a small ship with a large red flag flapping wildly in the wind. It seemed strange to her that it was heading directly toward the ship.

Shielding her eyes with her hand, she stared at it and asked with concern, "Do you see that, Sir?"

"I do," he answered with interest, standing beside

her.

Brie felt her anxiety rise when she noticed the huge cruise ship slowing down. "What do you think is happening?" she asked the others in concern.

"I'm sure they're just boat enthusiasts out for a joyride," Lea told her.

"But a cruise ship wouldn't stop for tourists," Brie insisted.

"It does seem highly unusual." Hunter agreed. "But I doubt modern-day pirates would attack a cruise ship."

"Maybe we should head back to the cabin just to be safe?" Brie suggested, clutching Antony to her chest.

Sir put his arm around Brie. "That won't be necessary, babygirl."

She was puzzled by his answer and asked, "Why, Sir?"

"Did you notice what's on the flag?"

Brie shielded her eyes again and squinted at the red flag. "Is that…?" Shaking her head, she murmured, "It can't be!"

"It is," Sir assured her.

Her heart began to race as she stared at the waving red flag with a black dragon in the center—a symbol she was quite familiar with. Turning to Sir, she asked, "What's going on? I don't understand, Sir."

He smiled as he picked up Hope. "We need to head down now to disembark."

Surprised, Lea cried out, "Disembark?"

Sir smiled when he answered Lea, "The person on that ship has come to kidnap my wife and children."

Lea shot Brie a worried glance.

"That's Rytsar's family crest on that flag!" Brie explained excitedly.

Understanding flashed in her friend's eyes, but she still looked bereft. "Does that mean you're not coming back?"

Brie looked at Sir to answer.

"Rest assured, Ms. Taylor, we will meet you at the next port," Sir stated as he hurried Brie along.

The staff was quick and efficient as they helped transfer the four of them from the cruise ship to the boat through the same portal the cruise ship used for ferries. Brie could not hold back her tears of joy when she saw Rytsar standing on the deck of the boat, his arms spread wide.

"*Radost moya!*"

Sir took both children so Brie could run to Rytsar. She started to sob when he enveloped her in his powerful embrace.

"It has been too long," he stated gruffly, his thick Russian accent tinged with emotion. "It feels like a lifetime ago…"

Brie nodded, burying her head against his chest.

"Come, *moy droog*," Rytsar commanded, opening his arms to include Sir and the children in his immense embrace.

For the first time in what seemed like forever, Brie felt completely safe and at peace with the five of them together again.

It wasn't until Antony started squirming uncomfortably that Rytsar finally let go of them all. Brie noticed him quickly swipe his eyes.

"*Dyadya!*" Hope called out, reaching desperately for him.

The burly Russian's heart-warming smile touched Brie as he picked up her little girl and crushed her to him. "Oh, how I have missed you, *moye solntse*."

Hope searched her *dyadya's* face for a moment before grabbing his cheeks with her little hands and pressing her nose against his. It was endearing to see the big, intimidating sadist under the spell of their little daughter.

Brie studied Rytsar as he interacted with her daughter. She noted that his face was lined with exhaustion. Concerned, she laid her head against his muscular arm. "How long will you be with us?"

Rytsar frowned when he answered, "I cannot stay long, *radost moya*."

Heartsick, Brie cried, "Why not?"

"When your Master told me you were struggling after Marquis Gray's confession, nothing could keep me away." While still holding Hope, he grabbed Brie behind the neck, kissing her forcibly on the forehead. "It is imperative I return to Russia, but I had to see you in the flesh. My soul needed to connect with yours."

She felt the same need and wrapped her arms around Rytsar, never wanting to let him go.

Rytsar glanced at Antony and shook his head. "Sadly, time has not been my friend. *Moy gordost* is no longer an infant but a little boy."

Brie gazed at their son, suddenly appreciating how much he had grown in the time since she'd last seen Rytsar. That whole period of her life had become a blur after the kidnapping.

But seeing Antony through Rytsar's eyes revealed to her just how quickly time had slipped away.

"There is no time for sorrow," Sir stated firmly. "We are together and must make the most of the little time we have."

"*Da!*" Rytsar agreed, shaking off his melancholy. Still holding Hope, he took Antony from Sir. Bouncing both children in his arms, he growled enthusiastically, "I must get in all of my *dyadya* time while I can."

Brie stood next to Sir as the boat sped away from the cruise ship, following the coastline north.

"So, where are we headed?" Sir asked Rytsar.

He smirked in answer. "That is for me to know, *moy droog.*"

Sir furrowed his brows and reminded him, "I am not one of your subs."

Rytsar grinned, "But you are married to one."

Sir rolled his eyes. "Do you seriously need me to teach you a lesson in respect?"

Snorting, Rytsar said, "I would like to see you try, comrade."

Brie gazed tenderly at both men, loving their brotherly banter. She smiled as a feeling of contentment washed over her.

Sir took Antony from Rytsar when he began to fuss, and their little boy immediately quieted down. Sir leaned against the railing while he held his son, gazing at the ocean with a far-off look as the breeze teased his hair.

Brie wondered if Sir was thinking about his childhood and sailing with his own father. And then she caught something that gave her goosebumps.

Antony had lifted his head and was staring out at the ocean with the same expression on his sweet baby face, their profiles almost perfect mirrors of one another.

Father and son. Son and grandson. It was proof that the seeds Alonzo planted years ago continued to live on.

Brie glanced back at Rytsar, then smiled as she watched him tickle Hope's stomach. Her daughter's trills of joyous laughter filled the air.

If only this moment could last forever, she thought with a sigh.

Pretty Horses

The boat landed at a port in Baja California, Mexico, where a vehicle was waiting for them. Brie was curious about where they were headed when the driver drove east and they wound their way up some mountainous hills.

Rytsar couldn't stop smiling at Brie during the drive. "I know *moye solntse* will love this, but I suspect you may love it even more."

"Just a hint?" she begged him. "You know how I am about surprises."

He raised an eyebrow, answering with a wicked smirk, "I do."

"Patience, babygirl," Sir commanded, patting her knee.

Brie glanced down, sighing because she had a severe lack of it. It made her seriously wonder if patience was something she would ever master.

The driver finally turned down a long driveway toward a cluster of buildings. Hope began slapping the window excitedly, squealing when she saw all the different horses. "Horseys, Papa! Horseys!"

Sir smiled, kissing her on the head. "Yes, little angel, lots of horses."

When they pulled up to a large ranch house, Brie turned to Rytsar. "Is this a dude ranch?"

"*Nyet*," he chuckled. "This is a safe haven for abused and neglected horses."

Brie looked at him questioningly, surprised and touched to hear it.

Rytsar got out of the car and held out his hand to Brie as he explained, "They rehabilitate them so they can become working members of the ranch." He gestured to the expansive acreage dotted with large outbuildings. "But to keep the ranch running, they depend on the donations of others."

Brie scanned the rolling hills and was impressed when she counted over thirty horses. "Wow, this place is amazing!"

She jumped, startled by a loud snort at her feet. When she looked down, she was surprised to see a large pig sniffing at her feet. He looked up at her, wiggling his tail excitedly.

"Piggy!" Hope cried.

"Don't mind Nacho," someone called. "He likes to greet all of our guests."

Brie looked up to see an attractive woman emerging from the ranch house, her brown hair bound up in a ponytail. She was dressed in dusty blue jeans and muddy cowboy boots.

Brie instantly responded to the woman's pleasant

smile and easy demeanor as she walked up to Rytsar and held out her hand. "*Señor* Durov, I presume."

"*Da*," he answered, shaking her hand.

"I'm Rosita, the woman you spoke to on the phone."

"It is a pleasure to meet you, Rosita," Rytsar replied in his thick Russian accent. "I appreciate you honoring my request on such short notice."

Brie noticed the blush coloring her cheeks. She felt no jealousy toward the woman, however. She understood that it was a natural response when in the presence of the Russian.

She grinned. "I'm happy we could help, *Señor* Durov. And I have to thank you for the generous donation. It'll be put to good use here at the ranch."

"Of course. You are doing good work here." Rytsar stated, adding, "Such work deserves to be supported."

Rosita looked down at Hope and asked her, "Do you like horses?"

Rytsar swept Hope up into his arms and told her proudly, "*Moye solntse* is a great lover of horses."

Rosita grinned at Hope. "We not only have horses and ponies, but dogs, goats, sheep, chickens, and pigs on this ranch."

"Piggy!" Hope cried, pointing at Nacho.

"That's right," Rosita said, laughing lightly.

Turning to Brie and Sir, she explained, "All of them are rescue animals."

"Although I can't say I'm an animal person," Sir stated, "I appreciate what you are doing here."

Rosita smiled as she rubbed the top of Nacho's head. "Every creature deserves to be loved."

Hearing her response, Brie instantly thought of Master Anderson. It was definitely something he might say. She was certain the cowboy would feel right at home on this ranch.

"Are the accommodations ready?" Rytsar asked Rosita.

"They certainly are, Mr. Durov. Let me take you there."

They followed her to a lone cabin that was a distance away from the other buildings. Opening the door, she gestured to them to head inside. "I'm happy to say we were able to procure everything you asked for, as well as some quality vodka and pickles for your stay."

Brie scanned the cabin, charmed by its rustic style. It had plenty of modern luxuries, including a full kitchen and a fancy bathroom with a large shower, but the cabin's décor had a definite western flair.

Brie was quick to notice that the cabin had two bedrooms. Taking a quick peek in one, she was enchanted by the large bed with its beautiful ornamental iron frame, accented by a fluffy, white bedspread that reminded her of a cloud. It was inviting and promised all kinds of fun.

Brie glanced at Rytsar, who winked back at her.

"The kitchen is fully stocked," Rosita informed them. "However, you are welcome to join us for a community supper in the courtyard, if you like."

"Although I enjoy eating outside…" Rytsar answered, looking hungrily at Brie. He quickly added "…we'll be eating in tonight."

Brie felt heat rise to her cheeks under his intense gaze. She could already imagine the three of them enjoying the large bed.

"Very well," Rosita replied pleasantly. "I'll go and get the horses ready. If you need anything, please ring the house, and my staff will be happy to assist you."

After she left the cabin, Rytsar nodded to the bedroom and told Brie to open the chest of drawers she found in there. Brie grinned as she went to do his bidding, wondering what she would find.

Brie opened several drawers before she found it and let out a surprised laugh.

"Not what you were expecting, was it?" Rytsar asked in amusement, leaning against the door frame.

"Not at all!" She grinned, looking down at the three sets of clothes.

"If you go to the closet, you'll find more."

Brie walked over and opened the closet door. To her delight, she found boots for each of them, as well as stylish cowboy hats.

Looking back at Rytsar, she couldn't help but gush, "I can't think of anything more adorable than seeing you and Sir in these."

He raised an eyebrow and smirked. "I can." Nodding to her, he commanded, "Get dressed, *radost moya*. No panties allowed."

He shut the door, leaving her alone in the room. Brie went back to the drawer to get her clothes. Quickly shedding her sundress and sandals, Brie put on the jeans, plaid shirt, and leather cowboy boots, finishing her outfit off with the hat.

After tucking in the shirt, she looked into the free-standing mirror and grinned at herself. The pink gingham shirt was a lovely contrast to the blue jeans and complemented her white hat and brown leather boots. She definitely felt like a proper cowgirl in her outfit.

Walking out of the bedroom, she was met with the whistles of both men. And the moment Hope saw her, she cried out, "Mommy cowboy!"

"Isn't your mommy cute, little angel?" Sir murmured, walking to Brie. He turned his head at an angle to miss the wide brim of her hat as he went in for a kiss.

Rytsar stood back with his arms crossed, looking at her hungrily. "It is a good look for you, *radost moya*. I approve."

Brie twisted where she stood, smiling shyly under his intense gaze. "I can't wait to see you in your outfit, Rytsar."

With a half-grin, he bent down to pick up Hope. Handing her to Brie, he glanced at the room on the other side of the cabin. "*Moye solntse* has her own outfit. Why don't you get her dressed for the ride?"

Brie dutifully headed to the other room and found a frilly pink gingham dress for Hope, along with pink cowboy boots and a matching hat. Hope clapped her hands excitedly while Brie dressed her. She ran straight to the mirror the moment Brie was done.

Placing the pink hat on her head, Brie told Hope, "You are the cutest darn cowgirl I've ever seen."

Hope jumped up and down, then ran out of the room to show off her pretty clothes, crying, "Papa! *Dyadya*! Look at me…"

Brie was tickled to find there was even an outfit for Antony. She quickly dressed him too, smiling as she put on the tiny blue jeans, plaid shirt, and little brown socks that mimicked leather boots. Before she carried him out of the room, she placed the tiny hat on his head and secured the strap under his chin.

Excited to show Rytsar, Brie stopped dead in her tracks the moment she stepped out of the bedroom.

Her stomach did a flip-flop when she saw both Sir and Rytsar standing before her, dressed as cowboys all the way down to their sexy leather boots.

Sir looked incredibly handsome in his blue plaid shirt, dark jeans, and black hat. As did Rytsar, who sported a red shirt instead.

"Wanna take a ride on my…horse?" Rytsar asked with a sexy growl.

Brie was so turned on by the sight of the two dressed as cowboys that her pussy started getting wet. "Oh, my…" she purred, fanning herself.

There was a light rap on the door. "The horses are ready when you are, *Señor* Durov."

Brie looked down at her son and smiled, telling them, "I'll stay here and watch Antony."

"You'll do no such thing, *radost moya*!" Rytsar stated, opening the door. "Rosita has graciously offered to watch Antony during the ride."

Mateo, a ranch hand who introduced himself as their guide, walked them down to the stable. "The horses are saddled up and anxious to ride out."

Rosita was waiting for them at the stable doors. "I wanted to introduce you to your mounts."

Running her hands down the neck of a beautiful dapple-gray stallion, she said, "This is Pepper. He'll be your ride, *Señor* Davis."

"Really?" Sir replied, sounding surprised. "I thought stallions were too temperamental to ride."

She laughed. "Actually, stallions are commonly ridden in the rest of the world, and even preferred in some countries. While most of the world sees horses as 'partners', the riding culture in the US is distinctly different. For some reason, Americans tend to treat their horses as pets, and they prefer mares and geldings.

Sir patted the stallion, looking at the animal with respect. "I had no idea…"

"Pepper is a patient horse and an excellent partner," Rosita assured him, obviously proud of her horses.

Moving on to a buckskin with a long, black tail and mane, Rosita told Rytsar, "And this is your horse, *Señor* Durov. Don't let her name fool you. Sandstorm is as gentle and steadfast as they come. She'll be the perfect ride for you and your niece."

Rytsar picked Hope up to let her pet the horse's nose. "Feel how soft the muzzle is, *moye solntse*."

Rosita then moved to the last horse, a chestnut beauty with a white rump speckled with spots. "*Señora* Davis, you will be riding Wildflower. Of course, all of our horses are special, but Wildflower is especially unique."

"How so?" Brie asked, holding Antony up so he could touch the horse's soft coat.

"Wildflower was found abandoned and starving in a field, along with four other horses. Of the five, Wildflower was the most emaciated—all skin and bones and barely able to walk." Rosita looked at the horse with sympathy, shaking her head. "When they brought all of the horses to our ranch, I decided to keep them together to help them assimilate easier."

Stroking Wildflower's nose, she said, "Unfortunately, Wildflower was not interested in eating, and I was afraid she wouldn't survive more than a couple of days. But after watching her more closely, I noticed something unusual about her. It seemed as if Wildflower wasn't avoiding eating but saving the food for the other four mares. She wouldn't go near it until the others had eaten all of their feed. To test my theory, I separated Wildflower from her herd and fed her in a stall. When she was alone, Wildflower gobbled up all of her feed." Shaking her head, Rosita told Brie, "She even tried to eat the bucket once it was all gone."

"Poor thing!" Brie cried, petting the horse's neck.

Rosita nodded sadly. "It wasn't until then that I realized Wildflower had set aside her own needs to help the other horses in her herd to survive."

"Wow," Brie exclaimed, looking at Wildflower with new respect.

"Sadder still, we discovered that the horses hadn't been abandoned as we'd assumed. Their owner, a solitary woman who lived in the backcountry, was found dead out in her field. Based on the condition of the body, the police believe the horses had been on their own for months scavenging for food in the desert."

"It's a miracle they survived!" Brie exclaimed.

Rosita nodded. "They all survived because of Wildflower."

Brie was touched by the compassion and strength she saw in Wildflower's big brown eyes. "Thank you for choosing her for me."

Rosita smiled warmly. "My pleasure, *Señora* Davis."

"Shall we mount up?" Mateo called out.

Brie kissed Antony on the cheek before handing him over. "If he gets fussy, he likes to be rocked. He also likes to be sung to, but if that doesn't work, you can try…"

Rosita chuckled. "I have three grown sons. I'm sure I can keep Antony entertained while you're gone."

Brie smiled. "I'm sure you can."

"Let me help you on your horse, *radost moya*," Rytsar told her.

Giving Antony one more kiss, Brie took Rytsar's hand and let him guide her up and onto Wildflower. Brie smirked when she felt Rytsar's hand press against her pussy as he "helped" her onto the horse. Handing her the reins, he gave her a private wink.

Turning to pick up Hope, Rytsar tweaked her nose "You are riding with your *dyadya*."

"Yay!" Hope squealed.

Brie glanced at Sir and watched in astonishment as he mounted the stallion in one fluid motion. "I didn't know you knew how to ride, Sir."

Sir tipped his hat. "I have Anderson to thank for that."

Mateo led the way as they headed out and onto the trail. Brie looked back, waving at Antony, who took no notice of her. He was too captivated by the flock of chickens that had gathered around Rosita.

Brie turned to face the trail, excited about their adventure ahead.

Mateo took them on a leisurely trail that wound through the desert hills.

It was a perfect day to ride, Brie thought as she looked up at the blue sky dotted with wispy clouds. The temperature was warm, but not overly hot.

Brie patted Wildflower in appreciation. The appaloosa was a beautiful horse, but Brie had completely fallen in love with her after hearing her story. She admired Wildflower's inner strength and willingness to sacrifice herself for the good of her herd. Seeing how healthy she was now, no one would ever have suspected the suffering she had endured or the physical and emotional scars she must carry.

Wildflower had the look of a prized champion but had the temperament of a gentle and compassionate soul.

Brie glanced at Sir. He looked sexy as hell riding the stallion. The horse walked with his head held high and his ears twitching constantly. It was as if Pepper was observing everything around him. Watching Sir ride with such confidence on the stallion was a definite turn-on.

Wanting to capture the moment, Brie pulled out her phone and took several pictures.

Sir noticed and smiled as he pulled his horse up alongside hers. "I have to say, you look irresistible riding that horse, babygirl."

"I was thinking the very same thing about you, Sir."

Wanting to get a video of Hope riding with Rytsar,

Brie aimed her phone and turned on the video. Rytsar looked handsome riding the buckskin. She would never forget her time spent with him on his horse Voin, riding in front just as Hope was riding now.

He had his strong arm wrapped securely around Hope, who was looking adorable in her frilly pink dress and cowboy hat. Rytsar must have sensed Brie watching him, because he turned his head. "*Moye solntse* is a natural-born rider," he stated with pride.

In response to hearing her name, Hope lifted her head to smile up at him.

Brie was grateful she was able to capture that precious moment on film. She decided to stop briefly to take photos of the two men riding together, not quite believing that any of this was real.

Afraid of falling too far behind, Brie put her phone away and leaned forward, patting Wildflower, before nudging her steed to catch up with the group.

When the guide finally turned them around to return to the ranch, Brie's heart rate sped up. Although this time spent out in nature riding these beautiful horses had been a fantasy come true, Brie knew she was about to experience a whole different kind of fantasy.

And things were about to get a whole lot hotter!

Cattlemen Heat

After Brie and Hope said their goodbyes to the three horses, they headed back to the cabin. Brie deeply appreciated her view as she walked behind Sir and Rytsar. There was nothing quite like the fit of tight jeans...

When they returned to the cabin, they found Rosita in the kitchen. She smiled as they entered and quickly wiped her hands with a towel. "Your son just went down for a nap a few minutes ago. He was fascinated by our menagerie of animals and refused to leave them until just now. The poor boy tuckered himself out."

"No problems, then?" Sir asked her.

"Not at all, Mr. Davis. He is a pure delight, and the animals love him."

He smirked, glancing at Brie. "He must take after his mother, then."

Hope, who had been full of energy and babbling on and on about the horses, suddenly started to cry. Despite Brie doing her best to comfort and distract her, the little girl could not be consoled.

Rosita offered Brie a sympathetic look. "She must be hungry."

Picking up a plate of little corn cakes, she offered it to Hope. "Would you like some gorditas de la villas?"

When Hope saw the treats on the plate, her whining instantly ceased.

"They're yummy," Rosita assured her.

Hope toddled over and picked one up, a little sob escaping her lips as she looked up at the woman tearfully. But, as soon as Hope took a bite, her eyes lit up and she reached out to grab another.

Rosita nodded. "That's right. Take as many as you want, *niñita.*"

Thank you, Brie mouthed to Rosita.

The woman winked in response and watched in satisfaction as Hope joyfully stuffed her mouth. When her tummy was full, she toddled back over to Brie and crawled into her lap.

Rosita smiled tenderly at their daughter, then turned to Rytsar. "I trust the ride went well, *Señor* Durov?"

"It was perfect," he answered. "I commend you on your rehabilitation of these fine animals. You've taken spirits that were broken and successfully brought them back from the abyss to live productive lives."

"It's a true passion of mine, *Señor* Durov."

"That is evident." When Rosita started toward the door, Rytsar stood up and opened it for her, following her outside. "I do have one question for you…"

Sir looked at Brie, flashing her a captivating smile. "How are you doing, babygirl?"

"I'm on cloud nine, Sir. Being together like this has lifted my spirits more than I can say."

He nodded in agreement. "I feel the same. There's a synergy between the three of us that extends to the children."

"Yes!" Brie kissed the top of Hope's head. "It's as if we're all on the same frequency, and the resonance it creates is powerful."

He looked at her thoughtfully for a moment. "I felt that vibration when I first met Durov, but it wasn't until you entered the picture that the resonance happened."

Brie was deeply moved by his statement.

When Sir went to take his hat off, she begged, "Could you leave it on just a little longer?"

Smirking, he tipped his hat in answer.

Brie sat in silence, gazing at him lustfully. Truly, Sir was a fine specimen of a man, whether he was dressed in cowboy gear, a business suit, or…nothing at all.

When Hope's head began to nod against her chest, Brie looked down and saw that her little girl was struggling to keep her eyes open.

"And another one bites the dust," Sir chuckled. Picking up Hope, he carried her off to join Antony in the other room for a mid-afternoon nap.

Adjusting his hat on his return, Sir told Brie, "It's still early, but I think the three of us should take advantage of this unexpected gift."

"I agree, Sir. One hundred percent," she answered, excited at the prospect.

Brie was surprised when Sir's tone suddenly became deadly serious as he sat down beside her. "It's important that you honor your safeword today. I know it would be easy for you to ignore your own needs in a desire to please us. But this is the first time the three of us have scened together since you were rescued, and neither Durov nor I wish to undo the progress you've made."

She smiled, reaching out to take his hand. "I know that, Sir. I completely trust you both."

He squeezed her hand, looking at her intently. "Which is why *we* need you to be honest with us during the scene."

"I promise, Sir." Brie laughed lightly. "Actually, I've been desperate to connect like this."

Squeezing her hand again, he said, "I just wanted to remind you, babygirl. In case you get caught up in the moment. Your well-being is the only thing that matters to me."

Tears of gratitude welled in her eyes. "I love you, Sir."

Rytsar swung the door open, waltzing back into the cabin with a huge grin on his face.

"You look like the cat who ate the canary," Sir said with a laugh.

"I am having a very good day, comrade" he announced.

Nodding at Brie, Sir told him, "The children should be asleep for quite a while, so we thought—"

Rytsar clapped his hands together, "Excellent plan!" He suddenly glanced at the children's door with a worried look, adding in a low voice, "I will pour the vodka. You get the pickles, *radost moya.*"

She hurried to the kitchen and searched the cupboards until she found the jar of pickles. Laying them out artfully on a plate, she felt giddy knowing the three of them were about to scene together after being apart for so long.

After a round of vodka, Rytsar stood up and held out his hand to her. "Would you like to dance in the sheets with two cattlemen?"

Brie smiled as she took his hand. With a wicked grin, Rytsar led her into the bedroom on the opposite side of the cabin, with Sir following beside her.

Knowing exactly what she wanted, Brie sank to her knees between both men and bowed her head before asking, "May I undress you both, Master?"

"Yes, téa," Sir answered, his voice low and seductive.

Gracefully standing up from the ground, she started by undoing Rytsar's shirt, enjoying the elegance of the pearl snap buttons. Not only did they look classy, but each time she undid one, it made a satisfying snapping sound.

She looked up and murmured to him, "I love a good snap…" Brie slowly undid each one and pulled his shirt open, exposing the dragon tattoo on his muscular shoulder. Brie hadn't realized how much she'd missed Rytsar's unique scent until now—the mixture of earth, spice, and leather.

Closing her eyes, she took a moment to breathe in the smell of him.

Leaving light kisses on Rytsar's chest, she slipped his shirt off and folded it before laying it down on the floor.

Turning to Sir, she bit her bottom lip as she took her time unsnapping each button. Opening his shirt wide, she ran her hands over his toned chest, purring in delight.

After removing Sir's shirt, she knelt down on the floor to take off his cowboy boots next, setting them neatly beside her before taking off his socks. Brie then went for his belt, enjoying the metallic clinking sound as she removed it.

Looking up at Sir from under her wide-brim hat, Brie maintained eye contact with him as she unfastened the button of his pants and slowly unzipped them, brushing her fingers against the rigidness of his shaft.

Brie grabbed the waistbands of both his pants and boxers and inched them down. Then, just as she had with their shirts, she folded both items of clothing neatly and placed them on the floor with slow, deliberate movements.

She stared longingly at his handsome shaft for a moment before returning to Rytsar.

The Russian watched her with laser intensity while she undressed him, his cock visibly straining against his jeans. When she finally released it from the confines of his skin-tight Levi's, he groaned in satisfaction.

Tempted to kiss it but knowing she had not been given permission yet, Brie bowed her head in an open kneeling position and waited.

"Pleasure our shafts, téa," Sir commanded.

Breathless with anticipation, she answered, "Yes, Master."

Taking off her hat, she placed it on the floor. Then she wrapped one hand around each of the shafts of her two cowboys and stroked them at the same time.

Brie went from one to the other, licking and teasing the head of their cocks with her mouth. She moaned in pleasure, her pussy gushing, when she tasted the light tang of their precome.

"More of you, *radost moya*," Rytsar growled.

Still stroking Sir's cock, Brie wrapped her hand around Rytsar's shaft, encasing his cock with her lips, and began to suck. He grasped the back of her head and grunted in pleasure.

Urged on by his excitement, Brie relaxed her throat to take him even deeper. Gripping Sir's cock tighter to mimic the pressure of her throat, she stroked him in sync with the movement of her mouth as she deepthroated Rytsar so what Sir was seeing would match what his shaft was feeling.

"Fuck…" Sir groaned deeply in appreciation.

It was empowering to please both men at the same time in this way, and she loved the decadence of being able to switch cocks at her pleasure. After twirling her tongue around the head of Rytsar's cock, she immediately turned and did the same to Sir's.

Soon, it was Rytsar's turn to watch as she deepthroated her Master. She stroked Rytsar's cock to match perfectly in pressure and rhythm, and tasted more of his precome.

It didn't take long before he commanded hoarsely, "Enough!"

She knew he was riding too close to the edge after being separated for so long. She immediately stopped, not wanting to take him over that precipice.

Sir reached down and lifted Brie's chin. "It's time to

undress you now."

Brie whimpered in anticipation as she stood up, goosebumps rising on her skin when both men approached her. They were still wearing their cowboy hats, which fed into the uniqueness and excitement of this fantasy.

The unfamiliar environment and the prolonged separation only made this moment that much hotter!

Rytsar surprised Brie when he unsnapped the length of her shirt in one fluid motion. The sound and feel of it made her heart race. He tossed her shirt to the floor, then reached between her legs. He chuckled knowingly when he found her jeans soaking wet.

The two men made quick work of the rest of her clothing, leaving her naked and oh so aroused…

"Before we begin, I want to add another element to the scene, *moy droog.*"

"What's that?" Sir asked.

Rytsar walked to the dresser and pulled out three blindfolds.

Brie gave him a questioning look.

"*Radost moya*, do you remember our first encounter?"

"Of course," she answered, having never forgotten their first scene together when he had fulfilled her Warrior Fantasy.

"I stripped away all of your senses and then brought them back one by one. Do you know why?"

She shook her head.

"To heighten those senses and make you more aware. Because of that, when we finally connected, it was at a much greater depth."

Brie nodded, recalling how intense their first encounter had been.

Taking off his hat, Rytsar held up the blindfolds to her. "I hunger for a deeper level of connection."

She stared at them and felt a chill of fear, despite having worked through the trauma a blindfold had induced with Faelan.

"What are your thoughts, téa?" Sir asked, noting her hesitation.

"I want to, Sir. But I am feeling at a yellow right now."

"You can take the blindfold off at any time, *radost moya*," Rytsar assured her.

He handed the three blindfolds to her. "You will be in control."

She stared at the three blindfolds. Knowing she was not required to keep the blindfold on calmed her fears.

Smiling at them both, she stated. "I want to explore what it feels like to connect this way."

Sir nodded.

"Good!" Rytsar swept her off her feet, pressing her against his naked body as he carried her to the bed. He placed her down gently, stating, "I volunteer to be first."

Brie set the two other blindfolds down as Rytsar turned around. She felt butterflies when she covered the sadist's eyes with the black cloth, tying it securely behind his head.

Sir sat down on the opposite side of the bed. She crawled over to him and he leaned in for a kiss. She felt the surge of electricity pass between them as he pressed his lips against hers. Sir turned away from her so she could place the blindfold over his eyes. Her excitement increased as she adjusted the cloth once it was tied, making sure he couldn't see.

Taking a deep breath, Brie placed the final blindfold over her own eyes. She was surprised by the exhilaration as she blindly moved to the middle of the bed and then felt both men lay down on either side of her.

Instead of fear, Brie felt the thrill of exploration as she reached out to tentatively touch each man. Running her fingers lightly over their skin, she experienced a rush that only increased when she felt their hands on her.

Goosebumps of pleasure rose on her skin as Sir's fingers grazed her pussy while Rytsar teased her nipples. First, the two men explored her body with their hands, but soon they transitioned to lips, teeth, and tongues.

Having all three of them blindfolded at the same time left each of them vulnerable and open. It felt as if they were experiencing each other for the first time as she explored their bodies through her amplified senses, and Sir and Rytsar explored her.

The simple scene was wildly erotic on a level Brie hadn't experienced before.

When she felt Rytsar's tongue lick her clit, her senses were so heightened and her pussy was so on fire that she immediately came. She heard and felt him chuckle in satisfaction.

It seemed every touch, lick, and bite took on a surprising and complex note, leaving an indelible mark on her skin and soul.

Brie cried out in insatiable need when the men got into position to claim her. After experiencing the intensity of their touch on her body, feeling them inside her would be pure ecstasy.

Rytsar rolled her on top of him and pressed his hard cock against the wet lips of her pussy. She heard and smelled the lubricant as Sir coated his cock, and she felt the warmth of his touch as he positioned himself to take her.

Both men waited, extending this beautiful but torturous moment until she begged them to take her.

"As you wish…" Sir murmured in her ear.

Brie held her breath as both men pushed their cocks into her at the same time, spreading her wide with their girth. She gasped, accepting and savoring the pleasurable pain of it.

Rytsar pressed his lips hard against hers, exploring her mouth with his tongue while the two of them thrust into her repeatedly.

Knowing her body well, the two men moved as one, completely in sync with each other. There seemed to be an otherworldly aspect to their claiming because of the intensity of their senses and the connection the three of them shared.

Tears soaked her blindfold as she lost herself in the sheer beauty of their possession. Each thrust increasing her level of sensitivity and causing her climaxes to grow more powerful.

When both men finally came, Brie not only felt their cocks pulsing as they released inside her, but she felt the warmth of their come and could smell her wetness mixed with the erotic scent of each man.

She shuddered in pure ecstasy, her entire body trembling as her inner muscles caressed both their shafts, announcing her final orgasm.

Afterward, Brie lay there still riding on the subhigh.

She felt Sir slip out of the bed and lifted her blindfold. She watched him throw on a pair of sweatpants.

"I'll watch the children so you two can have time alone."

Rytsar removed his blindfold, nodding. "Thank you, *moy droog*."

Brie scooted to the edge of the bed and clasped Sir's hand, squeezing it tight. He lifted her hand to his lips before leaving the room.

Alone together, Brie turned in the bed to face Rytsar. "I have missed you terribly."

With a penetrating gaze, his blue eyes bore into hers. "I cannot express how difficult it has been to remain in Russia."

She stroked his clenched jaw. "Then stay."

"I cannot. The creature is cunning and has eluded my best men thus far." A devious smile spread across his face. "But I know exactly how to reel her in. The wheels have been set in motion and I cannot delay."

He met her gaze, telling her, "It was foolish of me to come…but my soul would have withered to dust if I had not."

His words tore at her heart. "I'm sorry."

Rytsar shook his head. "Do not apologize, *radost mo-ya*. I am here because I love you."

"I love you, too!" she said, wrapping her arms around him.

Brie felt his pain when he confessed, "I know you

have been through hell and it breaks me inside."

Tears filled her eyes, the dark memories of her captivity suddenly swirling inside her. Still, she refused to let them overpower her. "I'm healing, Rytsar. He did not break me."

He crushed her in his arms, a sob escaping his lips. She knew he had suffered every second since her kidnapping and still worried she might not survive, because of what had happened to Tatianna.

The two lay in each other's arms in profound silence, their souls communicating volumes in a way that mere words could not.

Brie woke up just as the light of a new day was coloring the sky. She smiled, feeling an overwhelming sense of joy. This time on the ranch had been soul-affirming and seeing Rytsar again had filled a missing piece inside her.

It felt so natural and right, the five of them together like this—a family.

Stretching her arms, she turned in the bed and saw Sir sleeping peacefully beside her. Assuming Rytsar had gotten up early, she slipped out of bed and tiptoed to the door.

The instant she left the bedroom, she felt the emptiness and knew he was gone.

Scanning the cabin for any signs of him, Brie noticed an envelope sitting on the coffee table. Walking to it, she saw her name written in his handwriting.

"No…" she whimpered. She felt heartbroken that she hadn't had the chance to say goodbye. Picking up the envelope, she fought back tears as she opened it.

Radost moya,

Trust me, it is better this way.

Saying goodbye would have been too cruel and I could not have survived your tears.

It has been a blessing and a curse to be near you today. I am whole again but my heart aches even more.

I know the sacrifices I make now will provide you with a secure future. That is what I continue to strive and fight for. Remembering the joy on your face during our time together will warm me on the cold Russian nights ahead, and I am grateful.

I leave you with these words from the Russian poet, Innokenty Annensky.

And when oppressive doubt I must fight,
Her answer only have I sought and heeded.
It's not that she is emanating light:
It's that with her around no light is needed.

You will forever have my fidelity, protection, and comradeship,
Anton

Marquis

It only took an hour to drive down to the port of Ensenada to meet up with the ship. Because of Rytsar's thoughtfulness, the children were quiet the entire drive down as they made their way to the Baja coast.

Hope was entranced by the colorfully painted Russian toy Rytsar had left for her. It was a wooden paddle with little chickens on top. Whenever she moved the paddle, the ball underneath would pull on different strings, making the chickens "peck" the ground.

As for Antony, he was thoroughly entertained by chewing on one of the Russian alphabet blocks made out of cloth. Nadia, the lovely old woman who'd taught Brie how to make *Mamulya's* honey cake, had sewn the blocks by hand for their son.

Brie was grateful Rytsar's gifts had distracted the children from the abruptness of his departure. As for her, Rosita had handed her a manila envelope that morning before they left with the driver, telling her it was a gift from Rytsar.

Brie had chosen not to open it then because she was afraid that she might break down in tears in front of the children. She was still struggling with the fact he was gone but held on tightly to the hope that Rytsar would be successful in his mission to capture Lilly, and this latest separation would not be for long.

Staring down at the manila envelope on her lap, Brie told Sir, "More than ever, I understand what Shakespeare meant when he wrote, 'parting is such sweet sorrow.'"

Sir reached over and patted her knee. "Durov certainly made good memories to carry in your heart."

She nodded, then looked down at the envelope again. "I think I'll keep this as a pick-me-up for when I need one in the future."

"That is an excellent idea, babygirl." Raising an eyebrow, he praised her, "It seems you are learning patience after all."

Brie giggled. "Who knew such a thing was even possible?"

Once they arrived at the port, Brie, Sir, and the children boarded the ship to enjoy the last day of their vacation before returning home.

Lea and Hunter met them at their stateroom, and Lea immediately peppered Brie with questions. Keeping it light, Brie shared about the unique ranch and the incredible horseback ride.

"I can't believe Rytsar didn't stay longer," Lea confessed. "But I'm not about to complain because I've got my Stinky Cheese back," she squealed, giving Brie a squeeze.

Brie smiled, although her heart was silently aching.

Lea must have sensed her melancholy because she gave her another tight squeeze.

Hunter said, "People on the cruise have been buzzing nonstop about the modern-day 'pirate ship encounter', Mr. Davis."

Sir laughed. "I can only imagine the buzz that created."

Brie noticed Lea smirking at her, looking as if she was about to burst. "What?"

"I have the perfect pirate joke. Please, please let me tell it…"

Although Sir looked less than enthused, Brie played along, knowing Lea simply wanted to cheer her up. "Give it to me, girlfriend," she said encouragingly.

Lea let out a happy squeak. "Why is pirating so addictive?"

"I have no clue."

With twinkling eyes, she answered, "They say once you lose your first hand, you get hooked!"

Brie nodded in appreciation, giggling softly. "Okay, that is totally terrible, but it makes me laugh."

"I knew you would like it!" Lea declared. "I'll never let you down, Stinky Cheese."

Brie gave her a hug, adoring Lea's big heart and questionable humor. She looked over her friend's shoulder and caught Sir secretly smiling.

Lea for the win!

Brie was hesitant to leave this carefree time on the sea. She knew once they touched down on land in LA, she would be forced to face reality again. However, she was deeply grateful for this time away. It reminded her that beauty was abundant in the world even when there were times life became too stressful to see it.

As they were disembarking the ship the next day, Sir received a text. Brie knew something was up when he frowned while reading it.

"Is it from Marquis Gray?" she whispered.

He gave her a concerned glance, nodding as he slipped his phone back into his pocket.

Brie felt the anxiety kick back in again.

Rather than give in to the rising panic she felt, she whispered to herself, "Breathe…" Concentrating on slowing her breaths, Brie felt her crushing fear for Marquis slowly begin to lift.

Eventually, a smile spread across her face as she thought of Tono. She wondered if the Kinbaku Master knew how many times she'd depended on his powerful, yet simple, advice.

Noticing that Hope was struggling to keep up as they headed down the gangway, Brie picked her up and asked, "Did you have fun on the big boat, sweet pea?"

Hope nodded with a big smile.

"What was your favorite part?"

"Horseys!" she cried.

Brie laughed, kissing her on the cheek. "Your *dyadya* will be tickled to hear that."

On their drive to the house, Brie let out a sigh of relief mixed with dread. Being back home felt familiar and safe, but with it came all the fears she'd left behind.

Sir wrapped his arm around her. "Do you need time before we address this text?"

She shook her head. "Better to get this over with, rather than me wasting time dreading it."

"I agree, babygirl."

While the kids played with Shadow on the floor, Sir sat down with Brie in his office, explaining, "Gray texted that he would like to talk with you."

"Just me, Sir?" she asked in surprise.

He nodded, pulling out his phone so she could read his text.

Brie swallowed nervously as she stared at it.

"How do you feel about his request?" Sir asked.

She frowned. "I'm not sure."

"I can tell him you are uncomfortable with that arrangement."

She let out an uneasy sigh. "I trust Marquis." Thinking on it further, she felt more clarity and told him, "I would like to meet with Marquis, but…"

"What?" Sir pressed.

"I would like you to be near."

Sir nodded, his expression somber as he picked up the phone. Rather than text Marquis back, he dialed the number. Brie held her breath as she listened to a one-sided conversation between the two Masters.

Sir frowned slightly as he listened, then muted the phone and looked at Brie. "Gray is asking for you to meet with him today. He urges that it be sooner rather than later."

Although Brie was physically exhausted after their trip, she realized she would not be able to sleep until she heard what Marquis Gray wanted to say. "Tell him I'll come, Sir."

Unmuting the phone, Sir told him, "We can be there in two hours, Gray. Brianna will speak with you alone but has requested I be there."

After hanging up, Brie was concerned by his pensive expression.

"What's wrong, Sir?"

"Marquis doesn't sound like himself."

A chill ran down her spine. "What do you mean?"

He shook his head. "I can't put my finger on it, but something's changed."

Tears welled up in Brie's eyes at the thought of the beloved trainer being in pain.

"Are you having second thoughts?" Sir asked her when he saw a tear roll down her cheek.

She shook her head, wiping it away. "No. In fact, I'm more sure than ever."

Sir arranged for Mary to watch the children. When she arrived a little over an hour later, he explained, "I'm uncertain how long we will be, but the children are tired after the extended trip and I believe they won't stir until after our return."

"I can handle it if they wake up, Sir Davis," she assured him.

He pursed his lips, then looked at Brie. "I do not know what Marquis needs to share with Brianna this evening, Miss Wilson. But, whatever Brie may discuss with you on her return must be held in the strictest of confidence."

"I understand," Mary replied, adding solemnly, "It will go with me to the grave."

Sir sighed. "Hopefully, that won't be necessary. But I suspect Brie may require your support on her return. It was the reason I asked you to come. You are someone she trusts—that we both trust."

"Your trust is not misplaced, Sir Davis."

He nodded, then turned to Brie. "Are you ready, babygirl?"

She took a deep breath before answering. "I am, Sir."

When Mary walked over, Brie was expecting an encouraging hug. Instead, Mary socked her in the arm. "Whatever Gray confesses has no bearing on you."

Brie had never shared the details of Marquis's text with anyone and looked at her in surprise. "What are you talking about?"

"I had a hunch he might be involved with Holloway's death, and the fact he suddenly wants to meet with you only confirms it."

"I have no idea what Marquis has to do with that monster's death," she insisted.

Mary looked her in the eyes. "Whatever he did or didn't do was *his* choice. Remember that."

Brie nodded numbly, understanding what Mary was saying in academic terms. However, she could not bear it if Marquis Gray became another casualty of Greg Holloway's seemingly endless cruelty.

"I'll be right here, Stinks," Mary assured her as they walked to the door together. "This bitch ain't going nowhere—come hell or high water."

After meeting them at the door, Celestia escorted Brie to the study in eerie silence. Rapping lightly on the door, she said quietly, "Brianna Davis is here."

Brie trembled when she heard Marquis Gray command, "Come in, Mrs. Davis, and shut the door."

Turning to Sir, Brie forced a brave smile and put her hand on the doorknob. Celestia looked at her with concern but said nothing.

Goosebumps rose on Brie's skin as she entered the room and then quickly closed the door behind her. Keeping her head bowed, she moved to the chair that Marquis indicated and sat down beside him.

She was thankful for the fire burning in the fireplace. It helped stave off the chill that hung in the room.

"Mrs. Davis."

Brie could barely bring herself to meet Marquis Gray's gaze. But she dutifully lifted her eyes and braved staring into those penetrating eyes.

She gasped the moment their eyes met. She saw a darkness in them that she had never seen before, and she instinctively glanced away, her heart suddenly racing.

Startled by her reaction, Marquis assured her, "There is no reason to fear me, pearl."

Hearing his reassuring voice tugged at her heart, but she was still afraid to meet his gaze again.

"What are you frightened of?"

"You seem different, Asher," she murmured.

Marquis Gray lifted her chin with his finger, forcing

her to look at him. "You are right. What happened has changed me."

Brie gazed into his eyes, her heart aching when she saw the pain in them.

"It is not what you think, Brianna."

She looked at him questioningly. She suddenly realized she'd been holding her breath as she waited for him to explain.

His brow furrowed, lines of anguish cutting across his face when he confided, "I now live with the guilt. It is something I have never suffered before." His frown deepened. "I am plagued with overwhelming guilt because of what I failed to do."

Brie was startled by his answer. "What *you* failed to do?"

Anguish filled his eyes when he told her "I was the one who introduced you to Holloway."

"You had no idea, Marquis Gray. No one with any decency could imagine the things he was capable of."

Marquis shook his head. "I find it ironic that in my zeal to protect you as a student, I was quick to condemn Thane as Headmaster. Yet, I guided you into the hands of a monster."

"No one knew…" she whispered, her voice sounding strangled with her fear and self-condemnation. "If I had known the depths of his depravity, I would have fought tooth and nail to get Mary away from him instead of trying to advance my career by working with the devil."

"That is not your burden to bear, Brianna," he insisted. "It is mine."

He hesitated before continuing. "Having time to think on it, I've come to understand how exceptionally cunning and calculated Holloway was. It caught me off guard because I am normally a perceptive person. When I first met the man when we were younger, in the years before he became a huge mogul in Hollywood, I respected him for his vision and intelligence. Although we were never friends, I admired his obvious talent, and I supported him in the BDSM community."

He frowned, "I realize now that he became corrupted by his unprecedented success in Hollywood and, once he went down that path, I believe he purposely avoided all direct contact with me, knowing I would perceive the changes in him."

Marquis looked at Brie, his eyes flashing with anger. "I became a pawn. It was due to my favorable impression of him that I actively sought Holloway out to work with you and, in doing so, I allowed him to ensnare both you and Mary."

Snorting in disgust, he added, "For years, Holloway insisted on contacting me through hurried phone calls or by text. He used his hectic film schedule as an excuse not to meet with me in person. I never once questioned it…"

Brie's jaw dropped when she realized she had never seen Marquis speak directly to the man—except for the night of the award ceremony.

Remembering the terrified look on Holloway's face after Marquis had insisted he leave, then whispered in his ear. Brie asked Marquis the question she'd wanted to ask ever since that night. "What did you say to Holloway the night of the award ceremony, Asher? I have never forgotten the way his face drained of all color."

Marquis met her gaze, his eyes glowing with rage. "I was angered by his treatment of Miss Wilson that night and the utter disrespect he'd shown you…"

Brie instinctively shrank away under the intensity of his anger.

Seeing her reaction, he closed his eyes for a moment, reigning in his fury before explaining, "I took my inspiration from history. You see, there once was a famous English philanthropist who wanted to play a joke on fellow humanitarians he admired. He sent out ten letters which read, *'I know the dark secret you keep and will be contacting reporters on Monday.'*

"He thought it was a great lark because these men were highly respected and well-known for their kindness and generosity. He expected they would all have a good laugh over it, but when he failed to hear from a single one, he grew concerned and went to call on them. To his utter dismay and disillusionment, all ten had quietly exited the city without delay."

Marquis frowned, stating somberly, "It goes to prove that the majority of people you meet hold a dark secret they pray will never see the light of day."

The idea of that broke Brie's heart.

"Following the philanthropist's example, I simply told Holloway that I knew his secret and if he didn't leave immediately, everyone in attendance at the ceremony would know."

Marquis Gray's eyes darkened. "I should have realized his vileness went far deeper than I ever imagined."

Moved by his obvious suffering, Brie reached out to take Marquis's hand. "A person with a good heart is incapable of imagining that kind of evil. The fact that you could not is a testament to who you are."

Pulling away from her, he admitted, "I have recently been confronted by an extremely sobering fact. A person cannot be truly good until they confront their capacity for evil. I had no concept of the depths of my own depravity until I was confronted with the brutal torture Holloway inflicted on his victims…on you. I have come to understand the ravenous need to kill another human being that it induced in me, and I longed to make Holloway endure the same intensity of suffering he inflicted on others."

Marquis Gray narrowed his eyes, his voice chilling her to the bone. "I not only thought about it, but I also envisioned every gory detail in my head."

Brie felt immense sympathy for the beloved trainer.

Marquis looked away from her in shame. "I had no idea I was capable of craving such vile things until now." He let out a tormented sigh. "I find it abhorrent, Brianna, but it is a part of me."

She said with compassion, "You are a good man!"

He laughed ruefully. "I *thought* I was a good person, but I have come to the conclusion that unless a person can control the beast within, they can make no moral claims of being good."

Balling his hands into fists, he said in a strained voice, "I am now forced to control my urge to destroy, but make no mistake, Brianna. I am capable of great harm."

"I don't believe it," she insisted.

He confessed in a tortured voice, "I went to speak to him in maximum security. I *needed* to confront Holloway in person…"

Brie struggled to breathe, afraid to hear what Marquis would say next.

"Holloway was informed I was coming and I was surprised when he actually agreed to see me. When I arrived, I was impatient as I waited for the guard to fetch him."

Shaking his head, he told her, "I have never felt such a dark rage, knowing the atrocities he was responsible for and how profoundly people had suffered. When Holloway finally sat down on the other side of the glass, I had to briefly leave the visitor's room and then return to keep from breaking the glass between us with my bare fists."

His eyes darkened. "The moment the monster met my gaze, I saw him cringe."

Brie couldn't imagine facing the sheer force of Marquis Gray's anger.

"I managed to keep my voice calm when I confronted the man," Marquis continued, snorting in disgust. "Although he responded with a malignant smile, I could see the fear in his eyes when I told him, 'There is no escape for what you have done.'"

Darkness

After speaking with Marquis Gray, Brie left the study in a daze. Sir frowned when he saw her emerge from the room and stood up from his seat. "Is everything okay, Brie?"

She shook her head.

"Can I get you something, sweetheart?" Celestia offered, her voice small and anguished.

Shaking her head again, Brie reached out her hands as she headed to the couch, her movements sluggish as she sat down. She was too distracted by the conversation with Marquis Gray, his words still swimming in her head.

But when she looked up at Celestia standing over her with concern, she felt an overwhelming sense of compassion for her friend. "He is in a dark place, Celestia, but you already know that."

Tears came to Celestia's eyes when she nodded. "Yes…"

Brie said with a reassuring smile, "He shared with me how much he depends on your strength."

Celestia's bottom lip trembled. "I love him so much."

Brie nodded, appreciating the depth of that love. "He wants to protect you, Celestia." She glanced up at Sir. "To protect all of us. That's the reason he remains silent and withdrawn."

"What is he protecting us from, Brianna?" Celestia whimpered, the fear apparent in her eyes.

Brie glanced away for a moment and sighed deeply before meeting Celestia's pleading gaze again. "From himself."

She crinkled her forehead in confusion. "What do you mean?"

"Marquis told me he is experiencing something he described as a 'dark night of the soul'."

Celestia gasped, her gaze darting toward the door of the study. The soft cry that escaped her lips gave Brie goosebumps.

"What does that mean?" Sir asked Celestia.

When she turned to answer Sir, it looked as if her heart was about to break. "Hazrat Khan once described the 'dark night of the soul' as a total annihilation of all that you believed in and thought you were." Bowing her head, Celestia cried out, "My poor Master…"

"I assume this has everything to do with Holloway?" Sir asked Brie.

She nodded sadly. "Marquis Gray is being consumed by it."

Sir frowned, glancing at the study. "I can't imagine being in Gray's shoes right now, but I am certain he will find a way through the darkness."

Celestia asked Brie in a voice tinged with desperation, "Did my Master tell you what happened exactly?"

Brie shook her head. "He would only tell me the barest of details. He is keeping something back."

Celestia shot Sir a worried glance.

Concerned, Sir headed to the study and rapped loudly on the door. "Gray, I wish to speak with you."

"Go away, Mr. Davis," he answered, his tone firm and cold.

Sir glanced down, letting let out an exasperated sigh. Choosing to respect Marquis's wishes, Sir called out, "I'm a phone call away if you want to talk."

Brie stood up and wrapped her arm around Celestia, remembering how difficult it had been when Sir faced his own demons concerning his mother. It had strained Brie's new relationship with him to the point of almost breaking them—until Marquis Gray stepped in.

Walking back, Sir took a seat on the couch. "Celestia, we stand in complete support of both you and Asher. Anything you need, you call me—day or night."

"My Master is a righteous man," Celestia stated emphatically, her hand hovering over her heart. "Whatever he has done, he did it out of love. I do not question his actions, whatever consequences come."

Brie understood Celestia's steadfast loyalty to Marquis Gray. She had no doubt that her unwavering love and devotion would help him navigate the darkness he was drowning in at present.

On the drive home, Brie was lost in her own thoughts. She contemplated everything Marquis had shared with her. The respected trainer was not only complicated but was also an exceedingly intelligent man with rigorously high standards. What she hadn't understood until today was that the standards he held for others were nothing compared to those he held himself to.

It was difficult to see a genuinely good person questioning their own motives and taking responsibility for something Holloway had orchestrated.

"How did he seem to you?" Sir asked, glancing over at her as they neared the house. "I want your honest opinion."

Brie's heart ached when she told him, "He is struggling on so many different levels, Sir. It was frightening because Marquis Gray has always seemed so certain about who he is and what he believes in. He seems different now…"

"I can't imagine the internal battle he must be going through," Sir muttered, his voice deeply troubled.

Once they arrived home and he had turned off the car, Sir turned to face her. "I need to know. Did he confess to killing Holloway?"

"Marquis refused to answer when I asked him directly. He was firm about it not being a burden I should bear, then apologized again for sending that text that had inadvertently involved me."

Sir sucked in his breath, letting out a low growl of frustration. "While he is correct about not burdening you with it, he did reach out to me. But I'm left no closer to the truth than I was before. This is maddening!"

Brie's heart raced as she thought back on their conversation. "I'm afraid whatever Marquis did has turned his entire world upside down…and I'm not sure he'll ever recover."

Sir pushed his door open and exited the vehicle, slamming the car door shut. He was obviously upset but, by the time he had walked around to open her door, Sir had regained his composure, explaining, "It serves no purpose for me to get upset. Until Gray is ready to talk, there is nothing any of us can do."

Brie took his hand as he helped her out of the car. "What should I tell Mary, Sir?"

"Whatever you feel comfortable sharing, babygirl. The truth is, Marquis has given nothing away. It's just as you said. He is determined to protect us—even if it kills him."

Brie shivered, terrified at the thought.

"Forget I said that, babygirl. It was just a figure of speech," Sir told her, wrapping his arm around her. "Marquis is far too intelligent to do something foolish."

Mary was sitting on the sofa and looked up from the book she was reading, asking them in a casual voice, "So, how did it go?"

Although Brie was a jumble of nerves, she muttered, "Okay, I guess."

Mary closed her book, setting it down on the coffee table. "That bad, huh?"

Sir glanced around for the children. "Did either of them wake up?"

"No, Sir Davis. Those two have been sleeping like logs. I even checked on them a couple of times to make sure."

"Well, if that's the case, I will leave the two of you to talk." With a nod to Mary, Sir headed to his office and shut the door.

Mary frowned. "You're not looking so good, Stinks."

"I'm seriously worried about Marquis," Brie cried in a soft, frightened voice.

"So, he admitted to doing the deed, then?"

Brie shook her head. "No. He refused to give me details about the meeting, but Mary..." She glanced down, her voice trembling.

Mary drew closer, putting an arm around Brie. "What's going on?"

"Marquis is not well."

"What do you mean? Did Holloway do something to him?"

"Marquis feels responsible—for you, me, and every person that monster tortured."

Mary growled, "God, how I hate that Marquis got entangled in this by that fucking beast. Talk about polar opposites..."

"That's the thing, Mary," Brie whimpered. "He's changed. I felt it when I walked in the room. That suffocating anger he feels toward Holloway hovers around him like a dark shroud." Closing her eyes, she whimpered, "He can't become another casualty."

"He won't be," Mary insisted. "Our community will

never let that happen. He is too important to all of us."

From upstairs, Brie heard Antony's hungry cry and told her, "I'll just be a second."

"Nope. I'm going with you," she replied, heading up the stairs behind Brie.

When Brie entered the nursery, Antony instantly quieted.

"He's a real momma's boy, huh?" Mary asked.

Brie chuckled as she picked him up. "Truth is, I can't get enough of this little guy. He is perfect in every way."

"Not every way…" Mary complained, backing away. "Never could stand poopy diapers."

"What are you talking about?" Brie laughed. "You helped Celestia take care of Kaylee for months."

Mary pinched her nose. "Doesn't mean I liked it!"

"Antony, pay her no attention," Brie told him, rolling her eyes as she laid him down on the changing table. She handed him one of Nadia's alphabet blocks to play with while she quickly changed him.

Hovering near the door, Mary murmured, "I've been thinking about that little boy again…"

Brie turned her head. "The one from the compound?"

"Yeah. I read recently that he's still struggling to take a bottle and isn't gaining enough weight to leave the hospital yet."

"Poor little thing!" Brie cried, buttoning up Antony's sleeper before picking him up. Turning to face Mary, she asked, "Are you still thinking about adopting the baby?"

She snorted. "I'm too fucked up to ever be a mom, Stinks."

When Brie started to protest, Mary met her gaze evenly. Brie's words dried up in her mouth when she saw the torment brewing behind Mary's eyes.

"All I've ever known was abuse as a child, Brie. I don't have a fucking clue how to give the kind of love that little boy needs. But I can't stop hearing that tiny infant crying for his mother who would never come."

Brie hoisted Antony to her hip to give Mary a hug. "I know this may seem out of left field, but I wonder if you should try to find your real father."

"Are you fucking out of your mind?" Mary snapped, scaring Antony with the intensity of her outburst.

Brie bounced her son to calm him while murmuring to Mary, "Maybe if you connect with him, you can reclaim some of what was stolen from you."

"I know you can't be serious. Not after everything that happened," she growled.

Brie looked down at Antony. "I just know how I feel about this child. He is a part of me. Nothing could ever change that. Nothing!"

Looking tenderly at Mary, she added, "I can't help wondering if your father longs for that connection too."

"Don't you get it? My mother, my birth father, and that fucking bastard I thought was my father—not one of them wanted me."

The Letter

In serious need of a pick-me-up, Brie searched for the envelope that Rytsar had given her. Sitting at the edge of her bed, she took a deep breath before opening it.

Brie pulled out a photo of Wildflower and smiled, remembering the inspiring horse who was the embodiment of sacrificial love. She also found a certificate of adoption inside the envelope, as well as a title naming Brie as the horse's owner.

As per the adoption arrangement, Rosita would continue to care for Wildflower, but Brie was welcome to visit, love on, and ride Wildflower anytime she wanted. It warmed Brie's heart to know that Wildflower would remain with her herd under the loving care of Rosita and her staff.

Brie stared at the photo of the majestic animal and smiled. That day would be forever etched in her memory. Turing the photo over, she was touched to find a personal note from Rytsar.

Radost moya, the horseback ride is something I will always look back on with great fondness. To commemorate the day, and the beautiful horse who shares your fighting spirit, I have adopted Wildflower. She is your horse now.

~Anton

Reading his note brought happy tears to Brie's eyes. She kissed the photo before propping it up against the lamp on her nightstand. His gift was just what she needed to lighten her heart.

Brie pulled out her phone and texted him.

Thank you for my beautiful horse and the note.

She was surprised when he did not text her back right away, then glanced at the time and laughed at herself, realizing how late it was in Moscow. Brie wasn't sure she would ever get used to the time difference between them, but she took solace in knowing that her text would be the first thing Rytsar saw when he woke up.

With her spirits lifted, Brie decided to focus on something she was deeply passionate about.

Hitting dial, Brie waited patiently for him to answer.

"Hello?"

Brie's heart began to race when she heard the deep richness of his voice. "Master Nosh, this is Brianna Davis."

"I am busy at the moment, Mrs. Davis. What do you require?"

"I promise to keep it brief. You mentioned once that you were open to doing an interview with me. I wondered if we could schedule a time to meet. At your earliest convenience, of course."

He was silent for a moment.

Sweat started beading on her forehead as she waited for the head trainer's answer.

"Convenience is relative, Mrs. Davis," he stated, sounding slightly amused. "Although my schedule is booked up, I will have my secretary look at my calendar and contact you later."

"Thank you, Master Nosh," Brie squeaked before hanging up.

Lying back on the bed, Brie looked up at the ceiling and grinned. Although Master Nosh made her overly nervous due to his serious nature, the time she'd spent with him and his wife Nenove had shown Brie another side of the trainer that she admired and could relate to. It was because of their time together that she'd finally been brave enough to call him to schedule an interview. It just went to show that first impressions were only a snapshot of an individual.

Brie not only hoped to do justice with the interview she had planned for the revered head trainer of the Dominant Training Program but that she'd be able to reveal that other side of him to the audience, so they would come to understand the extraordinary man behind the serious exterior.

In her interviews with both Marquis Gray and Ms. Clark, Brie included a scene that displayed their skill as a Dominant. She hoped that Master Nosh would agree to do one as well, and she was super curious which instrument he would use.

Because he was so exceedingly private, Brie knew very little personally about the man, but this unique opportunity was about to change that. She felt incredibly lucky to have a career that allowed her to not only showcase the lifestyle she was passionate about but to also introduce someone like Master Nosh to the world—a man who possessed incredible skill and insight.

When Brie thought back on her first day at the Submissive Training Center, she knew that young woman would never have believed how far she would come as a submissive and as a filmmaker in Hollywood.

Brie smiled, imagining she was speaking to herself as she took a seat in Mr. Gallant's classroom on that first day.

"I'm so incredibly proud of you."

That evening, just as the sun was beginning to set, Brie headed to the kitchen to grab a snack and got the fright of her life. Out of the corner of her eye she caught a dark figure lurking at the back door, his image framed in the etched glass. Screaming in fear, she cried, "Sir!"

He burst out of his office. "Are you okay?"

She pointed at the door just as the person knocked.

Sir cautiously headed toward the door and then broke out in relieved laughter, telling Brie, "It's only Wallace."

She grasped her chest, willing her racing heart to slow down. "Thank goodness! I was afraid it might be…" She couldn't finish the thought.

Opening the backdoor, Sir said sternly, "You almost scared Brie to death."

Faelan wore a troubled expression on his face and Brie saw he was clutching a small white envelope in his hand. Sweeping back his hair nervously, he looked at Brie apologetically. "You mentioned I could visit when I come to the beach to watch the sunset."

She nodded, taking several deep breaths to calm herself. "That's right! I certainly did."

Addressing Sir, he asked, "May I come in, Sir Davis?"

Sir stepped back, gesturing for him to enter. After shutting the door, Sir asked him, "Is everything okay?"

He looked down at the letter in his hand and answered simply, "No."

Based on his odd behavior, Brie wondered if Kylie's parents were demanding custodial rights again. Concerned for him, she suggested he sit down in the living room.

"Where's your daughter?" Brie asked in concern.

"Mary's watching her," he muttered as he took a seat on the sofa.

When Faelan looked up at her, he looked completely devastated.

Goosebumps rose on Brie's skin, and she immediately took a seat beside him. "What happened?"

Faelan closed his eyes, not answering for a moment, and then sighed. "I went to visit Asher today. He hadn't been returning my calls, and when I talked to Celestia on the phone, I could tell something was seriously wrong. So, I asked Mary to watch Kaylee for me and headed over."

Faelan frowned. "Asher refused to see me, and nothing I said or did would change his mind."

Brie nodded. "Marquis is in a very dark place."

"I gathered that." Looking at the letter again, he explained, "I almost left their house empty-handed, but Celestia suddenly remembered that she had something that belonged to me and ran to get it."

He looked grief-stricken when he told her, "She said she ran across it while cleaning her desk, and apologized for not getting it to me sooner."

Brie's heart skipped a beat when she looked at the letter, afraid she already knew what it was. Mary had talked to her about it ages ago, but she'd forgotten all about it.

Brie noticed his hand began to shake as he clutched the letter tighter. "It's a letter from Trevor's mother. That's the boy I..." Faelan closed his eyes, forcing himself to say the word aloud, "...killed."

Brie looked up at Sir, silently asking permission before giving Faelan a hug. While she embraced him, she insisted, "You don't have to open it!"

Faelan was stiff and unresponsive, telling her, "It's my duty to read it."

"No, it's not."

"I agree with, Brianna," Sir interjected. "When dealing with my mother, I refused all communication because it served no useful purpose. You are not obligated to bear the anger and hostility of another person unless you choose to."

Faelan held the letter up and stared at it, telling Sir, "You don't understand. I never had the chance to speak to Trevor's mother because his father was so angry after the car accident that he threatened to get a restraining order if I came anywhere near either of them."

He looked down at the letter, letting out a tortured sigh. "She deserves to release the anger she feels. I killed her son and I ruined their lives in the most significant way a person can."

Sir nodded thoughtfully. "That may be true, Wallace. But what purpose does it serve for you to accept that anger when you are already remorseful and striving to make a better life for your daughter?"

Brie cried out, "Haven't you suffered enough?"

Faelan turned to Brie, silencing her with the intensity of his ocean-blue gaze. "Don't you think a mother deserves to be heard—especially when it involves her dead child?"

A lump formed in her throat and she reluctantly nodded.

Looking at the letter again, Faelan told them, "I have dreaded this moment ever since I saw Trevor's terrified face in my headlights just before we crashed into each other."

Brie couldn't imagine how horrifying it would be to know you had killed another human being, especially when it was someone so young. Bearing the guilt of knowing the accident was his own fault had to be heart-rending to Faelan.

Brie could understand why a mother would hate the person who caused the accident which killed her child. But Faelan was a good man and a father of a little girl now. He didn't deserve the setback this letter would bring, not after Kylie.

"Let me throw it away," she begged him.

Faelan looked into her eyes. "I don't need you to throw it away. I need your support."

Brie nodded, understanding it was why he had come to her. Sighing nervously, she accepted her role and grabbed his hand. "You've got my support."

Hope came down the stairs with Shadow following behind her. The moment she saw Faelan, she squealed in excitement.

Faelan froze, his emotions too raw to handle the innocent intrusion.

Reading the situation, Sir lifted Hope into his arms and headed back toward the stairs. "Let's read a book. You can pick your favorite one or let your papa surprise you."

Hope peered over Sir's shoulder, grinning at them both as he carried her back upstairs.

Once they were alone, Brie placed her hand on Faelan's shoulder and apologized for the interruption. "I'm sorry about that."

"No need to say sorry. It's not her fault I'm unstable and came here unannounced." Glancing back at the stairs, his voice softened when he told her, "It's good to see how happy your kid is. You and Davis are good parents."

"So are you," Brie reminded him.

Faelan let out a tortured sigh as a wave of grief seemed to wash over him. Brie suddenly realized that her words, which had been meant as a compliment, had only caused him pain.

"Fuck, I miss Kylie!" he groaned. "I wonder sometimes if her death was payment for Trevor. Ever since I killed that kid, my life has been a series of catastrophes."

Brie's jaw dropped. "You can't think like that! What happened to Kylie was a horrible tragedy, not some kind of 'payment' for your past."

Faelan shook his head. "To be honest, I still worry that our daughter might be better off with her grandparents. I could not bear it if I fucked up her life too."

"Faelan, you have to stop thinking like that. If this letter is making you think this way, I'll fucking burn it myself!"

His eyes widened in surprise. "I don't think I've ever heard you talk like that before."

Brie growled. "When I see my friend torturing himself over an accident that happened a lifetime ago, all because of a stupid letter…it makes me fucking angry."

Faelan's voice became eerily calm. "I have felt this way for a long time, blossom. I've had too many heartbreaks in my life not to believe that I'm the cause."

Her anger instantly dissipated the moment he used his pet name for her. It took her straight back to the beginning when she first met Faelan. He had been a tortured soul even back then.

Brie never forgot the day he confessed to her outside the tiny tobacco shop that she had been his reason for living again. But the truth was, it wasn't until he found

Kylie that he really began to live.

She realized now that when Kylie died during child-birth, Faelan had reverted back to that hurting young man, strangled with overwhelming guilt after the car accident. It was only through the concentrated efforts of both Marquis Gray and Rytsar that Faelan had been able to regain his former self-worth and was able to find the strength to become the kind of father his daughter deserved.

She stared at the letter with growing resentment. It seemed as if that damn letter was about to tear Faelan's life to sheds again and take his daughter's future with it.

Brie remembered Mary mentioned that Marquis Gray had insisted on Celestia not destroying the letter because he believed Faelan had a right to see its contents.

While Brie agreed with Marquis in theory, right now it felt like a terrible mistake.

Faelan waved the envelope in his hand. "I came to the beach thinking if I could connect with Kylie while watching the sun set, I would be able to handle reading this." He snorted in disgust. "It turns out, I'm too much of a coward."

"Trust your instincts," Brie begged him. "Throw the damn thing out now!"

He looked at her ruefully. "That's the thing, blossom. My instincts are to open it."

Brie closed her eyes, knowing there was no convincing him to do otherwise. Understanding what he needed from her, Brie wrapped one arm around him. "Open the letter, then. I'm not going anywhere."

With a sad smile, he nodded.

His hands shaking, Faelan ripped the top of the envelope open and pulled out a two-page letter. The stationary was embellished with colorful floral accents, making Faelan snort. "Seems ironic that she chose to use pretty stationary to pen a hate letter."

Undaunted, he unfolded the paper, taking a deep breath before he started to read it.

Brie looked away, not wanting to inadvertently peek at the private conversation meant for Faelan—although she was plagued with painful curiosity.

Faelan was silent as he read the letter, but Brie could feel the tension in his muscles growing with each passing second.

She heard the rustle of him moving to the next page as he continued to read. Brie felt his whole body start to shake. She turned to look at him, hoping to read his expression to discern how he was feeling.

He was staring at the letter, his face a deep shade of red and the veins in his neck pulsing in rage.

"What the hell did she say in that letter?" Brie cried angrily.

When Faelan met her gaze, Brie was paralyzed by the intensity of his anger. Thrusting the letter at her, he barked, "Read it yourself."

Faelan stood up and started pacing. Seeing how upset he was, Brie was almost too scared to read it. The woman's penmanship was beautiful, her cursive as pretty as the flowers printed on the stationary—which was disconcerting considering the effect her words were currently having on Faelan.

Dear Todd Wallace,

I have waited a long time to write you this letter. You see, my dear husband told me I was absolutely forbidden to ever write it.

Sadly, Cliff recently passed away. My heart has been broken a second time, but I am grateful for the precious years the two of us spent together.

However, as much as I still love and respect my husband, I've never felt right about keeping the secret. You need to know the truth.

Brie frowned and glanced up at Faelan. He was oblivious, pacing the house like a furious caged lion. Unsure if she wanted to know the secret, Brie had to force herself to continue reading.

Please understand, my husband and I had no idea. It came as a horrifying shock to us when we discovered what my son had hidden in our basement. I'm still haunted by it. All of those guns, the plans he had hung on the walls, and that goddamn journal.

As a mother, I can't imagine the pain Trevor must have been suffering to plan a horrific thing like a killing spree. I'd like to believe he would never have gone through with it, but there was far too much evidence to think otherwise. The sheer volume of guns and ammunition, as well as the detailed maps on the walls and the journal my husband found, leave me with no doubt that he was planning to carry out his deadly rampage.

Trevor not only planned to kill us but a number of students at the school as well. I truly think my son was psychotic.

Selfishly, I wish we had kept that door locked and never ventured down to the basement. It would have been so much easier not knowing, but it wouldn't have been fair to you.

You need to know that I forgive you for killing my son in that car accident. Although you were unnecessarily reckless, I know you had no intention of hurting, much less killing, Trevor. The fact is, that fatal accident saved countless lives, including my own.

Although I know this letter has been a long time coming, I hope it provides you with some comfort.

Sincerely, June

Brie stared at the letter in utter shock. "Faelan, I can't believe this."

He suddenly stopped pacing and walked over,

snatching the letter from Brie's hands. "They kept it from me this entire time!"

She shook her head, stunned that they would do such a thing.

"I'll never forget when Trevor's father sought me out at the hospital after the accident and yelled, 'There is nothing you can do or say that will ever atone for what you've done!' I felt so guilty for Trevor's death that I agreed with him. But before that asshole left my hospital room, he threatened that he was going to tell the whole world what I'd done and make me wish I had never been born."

Faelan snarled, "I can't tell you the hell my family went through. Trevor's father actively harassed my parents, making sure they suffered as much as I did because of my mistake. It finally got so ugly that my parents were forced to move."

He frowned, staring down at the letter. "It's the reason my parents now live in Colorado, alone up in the mountains. They didn't deserve that, and neither did my sister."

Faelan's face grew pained when he said, "Poor Lisa suffered the most…" He swallowed hard, looking as if he was debating with himself whether or not to voice what he was thinking out loud.

"I've never spoken about this with another living soul. Not even my parents know about it," he told her in a strangled voice. Faelan turned to face Brie, looking at her with profound sadness. "I almost lost her, blossom."

Chills coursed through Brie, understanding what he was implying. "Oh, Faelan…I'm so sorry."

"It wasn't bad enough that I carried the guilt of Trevor's death. Trevor's father was on the warpath and, because of what he did, my little kid sister tried to end her own life."

Slapping the paper with the back of his hand, Faelan roared, "This fucking secret they kept ruined my entire family and almost killed Lisa!"

Brie hugged him, wanting to comfort him. "Faelan, you were right to follow your instincts about this letter. If you had destroyed it, you would have no idea that you are a hero."

"I'm no hero," he growled.

"Just ask every kid whose name was written in Trevor's journal. I bet they would tell you differently."

Faelan sighed angrily. "I've spent my life trying to make up for killing a sixteen-year-old kid. Now, after reading this letter, I have no idea what to do or what to think."

Before he left, Faelan made her promise to keep the contents of the letter a secret until he chose to share it.

"I promise, Faelan, but can I tell Sir?"

For the first time that night, a slow grin played across his face. "Of course. I wouldn't want to be responsible for you having to kneel on rice again."

"I appreciate that." Brie chuckled lightly, grateful to see that spark return. She hoped, once he had time to process the magnitude of this new revelation, he would be able to reclaim that part of himself that he had lost.

Her Return

The next morning, Brie was surprised that Rytsar hadn't texted her back yet. She decided to call him directly, planning to give him a hard time about ignoring her. When his phone immediately jumped to voicemail, she wondered if he'd let his message box get too full again.

Sending him another text, she wrote:

Rytsar, why haven't you responded to my text? Aren't you curious to hear what I thought about my gift? Please give me a call as soon as you read this. I miss you.

Glancing at the picture of Wildflower on the nightstand, Brie smiled as she left the bedroom. Heading straight to Sir's office, Brie popped her head in and asked, "Sir, have you heard from Rytsar recently?"

He thought for a moment. "I haven't, actually. But then, I've been busy working on a project and haven't reached out. Is there a problem, babygirl?"

"I was just wondering because I texted him yesterday and haven't heard back yet."

"Durov did mention to me that he was planning to travel to Siberia for several weeks. If that's the case, he's probably out of range and hasn't received your text."

She nodded while a ping went off in her pocket. Glancing at her phone, she saw a new text suddenly pop up. Clicking on it, she read the text and smiled at Sir. "Guess who just texted me?"

"A Russian with a bad case of sadist humor?" he answered.

Brie grinned at his dry humor. "No, it's Master Nosh's secretary. She says he wants to meet with me to discuss the interview before they schedule it."

Sir nodded, smiling. "You will enjoy spending time with him."

Brie sighed nervously. "I'm sure I will, Sir, but the head trainer is so solemn. I find him a little intimidating."

He chuckled. "I can understand that. As a submissive, you respond naturally to his commanding presence, and his silence can be daunting unless you understand him. Nosh is a man of few words because he does not feel the need to speak unless he has something of importance to share."

Brie laughed. "If everyone were like him, the world would be a silent place."

Sir smirked. "And far more peaceful, I dare say."

"The thing I worry about is inadvertently offending him, Sir," Brie confessed.

He took hold of her hand and guided her to sit on his lap in his office chair. "Nosh reads people far better than I do. He can easily discern malicious intent from idle chatter. As long as you are open with him, you should have no issues, babygirl."

He chuckled and added, "I'll never forget the night I had to go to his office after failing to show up for a class because of my beast of a mother. It was grounds for immediate dismissal, and I fully expected my time at the Training Center to be at an end. But Nosh believed in me without any judgment. I trusted him enough to tell him what happened to my father—and the hell I'd endured because of my mother. As fucked up and crazy as my story sounded, he accepted everything I told him without question."

Hesitating a moment, he told her, "To have someone in authority believe me and want to help to lift me out of the mire I'd found myself in…" He shook his head with wonder. "It changed my life."

Brie felt goosebumps on her skin as she listened to his story. "I understand why you admire him so much, Sir."

Pressing his lips against hers, he murmured, "What he did for me eventually led me to you, babygirl."

"And I am eternally grateful to him for that," she said, kissing him back.

Brie was set to meet with the head trainer a half-hour before the Dominant Training class was set to begin for the evening. It was a super tight schedule, but it was the only time Master Nosh had open to meet with her.

Grateful for his willingness to squeeze her in, she made a point to arrive at the Center early so there was zero chance of offending him by arriving late. It also gave her a chance to chat with Rachael Dunningham.

Walking out from behind the receptionist's desk, Rachael gave her a hug. "I can't tell you how wonderful it is to see you again, Mrs. Davis!"

Brie gratefully returned her hug.

Stepping back, Rachael beamed. "When Master Nosh informed me you were coming, I did a little happy dance in my head."

Brie grinned at her. "It is lovely to see you, Miss Dunningham."

"How are the children?"

"Growing up way too fast, but that's the nature of children, isn't it?" Brie chuckled.

"Too true," she agreed. "You must be so grateful that terrible man is dead."

Brie suddenly frowned, Rachael's words immediately reminding her of Marquis Gray and his possible ties to Holloway's death.

"Oh, I'm so sorry, Mrs. Davis! I shouldn't have said anything. I didn't mean to upset you."

Brie reached out to give her another hug. "It's okay," she assured her. "I'm still raw after what happened, but you are absolutely right. Knowing that Holloway is gone brings me great solace."

After she let Rachael go, she told her, "I don't want you to ever worry about saying the wrong thing. I just want you to be yourself around me."

Rachael sighed, obviously still upset at herself, but she quickly nodded. "I am sincerely glad to see your smiling face and to have you visit here again."

"It's good to be back," Brie agreed.

Heading down to the bottom floor on the elevator, Brie reflected on her encounter with Rachael. She felt more confident about this meeting tonight after her talk with Rachael. It highlighted what Sir had shared about Master Nosh. When you understand someone's true intentions, the words they speak matter less.

Clutching her notebook to her chest, Brie knocked on the door of Master Nosh's private office.

"Come in," the head trainer called out, the tenor of his voice alone carrying great authority.

Just be yourself and don't forget to breathe, Brie reminded herself as she opened the door.

Walking into his office, she found Master Nosh sitting behind a rustic pine desk. It appeared he was a man of simple taste because the room was minimally decorated. The focal point of the whole space was the large painting on one wall.

Master Nosh got up from his chair to stand beside her and look at the painting. The first question he asked was, "Do you know whose portrait this is?"

Brie smiled as she gazed at it. "I do, Master Nosh. My Master told me about Little Wolf. He was the Cheyenne chief who brought his people back to their tribal lands against all odds. Sir told me he continues to be a constant source of inspiration for him personally."

Master Nosh nodded with satisfaction. "Sir Davis and I are alike in that way."

Studying the painting that Sir had talked so highly of was a treat for Brie. It felt like going back in time as she stood there staring at it, imagining what it must have been like for Sir when he was standing in this exact spot beside the head trainer while attending the Dominant Training course.

Brie studied the painting of the Cheyenne chief. It was exactly as Sir described, the confidence and intensity in Little Wolf's eyes made it seem as if he were a presence in this room. Even though it was merely a painting, the magnetism of the chief's persona beckoned to her. Brie was a firm believer that a person continued to live on in those they touched and through the difference they'd made while on this Earth.

"Please take a seat, Mrs. Davis. We have little time."

As she was sitting down, she said, "I'm grateful to you for fitting me into your tight schedule."

He made a rolling motion with his fingers, indicating she should get to the point of the meeting.

Brie laughed nervously as she opened her notebook.

"There is no point in feeling anxious, Mrs. Davis."

His statement was simple and profound. He was right. Feeling anxious did not serve any purpose. Accepting that truth immediately calmed Brie down.

She looked up from her notes and smiled. "Thank you for that reminder."

Starting right in, Brie hit the first item on her agenda. "Knowing your tight schedule, how long will you be available for the interview?"

"How long do you normally take for an interview?"

"I schedule them for an hour and a half, but I'm

happy to cut down the time for you."

"If that is the time it takes, then that is what I will plan for," he stated firmly.

"Excellent." She quickly noted it and then asked, "What time do you prefer, and is there a day that works best?"

"Before class begins would be the most efficient use of my time. As far as the day, it matters little to me."

Moving on to the next item, she asked, "Do you have any requirements for the shoot?"

He looked at her strangely.

Explaining, she said, "Like getting a list of the questions beforehand or topics you would like me to cover. Anything like that?"

"You are doing an interview, correct?"

"I am…" she answered with hesitation.

"Then you are in control of the interview, and I have no need for other requirements."

Brie bowed her head slightly, honored by his trust in her. Scratching the item off her list, she asked her final question. "In the past, I've filmed the trainers performing a scene. Is that something you would be opposed to?"

When he frowned, she immediately scratched it off the list.

Master Nosh looked at her in confusion. "Why would I mind? I am not ashamed of what I do."

She silently laughed at herself for making that assumption before listening to his answer. In the margin, she wrote, *He said yes!*

"I have to warn you that it will require another

shoot."

His frown deepened. "Can we not do it on the same day?"

She smiled. "Certainly, Master Nosh. I'm simply concerned since it would make a long day for you with an interview and filming a scene, on top of teaching your class, which doesn't end until midnight."

The head trainer looked nonplussed. "Matters of importance normally require sacrifice."

"I am deeply honored you feel that way, Master Nosh." Brie was awestruck by the head trainer's commitment to her documentary. "Can you give me an estimate of how much time you will need for the scene so I can add it to the schedule?"

"A half-hour..." he replied, then furrowed his brow thoughtfully and corrected himself. "No, make it an hour. I must allow enough time for adequate care afterward."

"Noted." Knowing her time was drawing to an end, she stood up, telling him, "That's all I had for you tonight."

"I have one thing I would like to add to this conversation."

Brie immediately sat back down. "Yes, Master Nosh?"

"Hollywood makes a poor habit of depicting the indigenous people of this country in a negative light. I agreed to this interview because I know that is not your intention."

She bowed her head in shame for what she knew her industry was capable of, nodding. "I'm mortified by the way the film industry has treated Indigenous Americans. It is a gross injustice that cannot and should not be tolerated any longer."

"Exactly," he stated quietly but with great force.

"Master Nosh, is there anything else you would like me to know before I leave?"

He shook his head and stood up, holding out his hand to her. "I look forward to the interview, Mrs. Davis."

Brie shook his hand firmly, her heart bursting with profound gratitude.

Riding on the high of the encounter, Brie immediately phoned Michael Schmidt once she had returned to her car.

"Mr. Schmidt, this is Brie Davis. I'm ready to begin working on the film again."

"It's good to hear from you, Mrs. Davis," the film editor said with a note of surprise in his voice. "If you believe you're ready for the pressure of this project, I should be able to gather the rest of the team first thing next week."

"Wonderful. I just finished speaking with the head trainer of the Dominant Training Course about an interview."

"Don't take his refusal to heart. Our team have approached him on several occasions and have been flatly refused."

She laughed. "I was hammering out the details with him today."

A pause. "Wait. You were able to get him to agree? I must hand it to you, Mrs. Davis. I didn't think he would ever entertain the idea."

"Thankfully, Master Nosh and I had an opportunity to spend time together recently. I believe his reservation about the interview may have come from his disdain for Hollywood."

Mr. Schmidt snorted. "Well, I can't blame the man for that. Hollywood has a long history of not treating Native Americans with any respect."

"Sadly, that is all too true. Thankfully, for you and me, Master Nosh is a man of remarkable character and can overlook the mistakes of the past in the pursuit of a promising future."

"I agree, that is certainly fortunate for us."

"While you start gathering the crew, I'll draft up questions for the interview so we can all go over them together next week."

"That sounds good, Mrs. Davis. I look forward to moving forward on this project." His voice then took on a more sympathetic tone when he said, "Let me just say that everyone here was horrified by what happened to you…"

Brie cleared her throat, suddenly feeling uncomfortable. "I prefer not to talk about it, but I do want to thank you for the numerous flowers you and your colleagues sent." That time being an emotional blur, she didn't remember any of the gifts that had arrived, but Sir had faithfully informed her each time one came to the house.

At her request, he'd had them sent on to a charity

that gifted the flowers to people recovering in hospitals throughout LA. She'd had no desire to keep the overabundance of flowers after her rescue since they'd made the house feel like a funeral home.

Mr. Schmidt laughed self-consciously. "I know it seems inadequate considering what you've endured, but it was important to our team that we show our support at such an extraordinarily difficult time."

"I sincerely appreciate your thoughtfulness and concern."

"Good, good," he said awkwardly, quickly changing the subject. "Would you like to meet at the office, or would you prefer us to come there?"

"At the office. I can't imagine everyone having to make a special trip here," she chuckled. Pausing for a moment, she added, "Mr. Schmidt, you don't need to treat me with kid gloves. I contacted you because I'm confident in my ability to jump back into the project. In fact, I crave the chance to start working on the documentary again."

"I appreciate your frankness, Mrs. Davis. And please call me Michael."

"Michael it is, then. See you next week."

Brie hung up the phone, feeling a surge of positive energy. This next film was going to be a triumph. Despite Holloway's efforts to silence her and her films, she would be the victor.

When she returned home, she swooped Antony up off the floor and twirled him in the air. "No one can take away your dreams, my son," she declared with a rush of excitement.

So, this is how it feels to be invincible!

Mystery Man

B rie had found the perfect frame for the photo of Wildflower. It was made of rustic wood that reminded her of the western cabin, but it also had metal filigree inlaid on the body of the frame, which reminded her of the bed they'd enjoyed together.

After setting the photo on her nightstand to admire it, Brie smiled to herself as she leaned down to open the nightstand drawer. A feeling of sentimentality washed over her as she picked up her beloved journal and began flipping through its pages.

Sensual memories flooded her mind as she recalled each fantasy she had penned in the journal and the scorching BDSM scenes that followed, which had incorporated the elements of those fantasies.

Brie vividly recalled the very first—her Warrior Fantasy.

That cherished scene had led to her first encounter with Rytsar. The Russian had fulfilled her journal fantasy, taking the essential elements of it and using them to create a unique scenario that made her fantasy spring to life. The scene opened her eyes to the power of fantasies.

She stopped on a page to read her cherished Wicked King Fantasy. Oh, Sir had been extremely clever with that one! He'd surprised her at the Commune when he'd played out the roguish scenario. Sir's skillful execution of the BDSM scene had pushed her limits and turned her simple fantasy into an erotic experience she would never forget.

Brie caressed the journal lovingly, enjoying all of the memories of those sexual fantasies being beautifully crafted into BDSM encounters. She felt the journal calling to her again…

It was another indication that Holloway's dark power was losing its suffocating grip on her soul. Taking her journal outside, Brie curled up in a chair and listened to the ocean waves crashing against the shore while she penned her next fantasy.

It's been far too long since I've been with a man. I have allowed the rigors of work to steal my time and zap all my energy.

I am an ambitious woman who wants to prove herself in the business world. But it's not just success I am looking for. I want to show every single person who ever doubted me that they were wrong—so fucking wrong—about me.

It's the reason I have accepted every project that comes my way, and why I will stop at nothing to make sure I succeed where others have failed. But I am beginning to realize something—there is a sinister side to being so driven.

I have ignored my needs as a sexual being.

By pouring all my energy to further my career, I have nothing left to give to myself when I have rare moments of downtime. Rather than invest energy in human interaction, I've relegated myself to a dependence on sex toys to satisfy my needs.

As gratifying as it is to orgasm on demand, my body longs for physical connection. I have an insatiable desire for it which grows with each passing day.

To honor those needs, I've chosen to do something radical.

I just turned down an opportunity with incredible potential. I now realize a sacrifice must be made if I am serious about putting my needs first.

I am well aware of the shocked expressions on my colleagues' faces when I choose to leave the office at five on the dot, rather than just before midnight.

Once I set my eyes on something, I am laser focused.

For the first time in a long while, I take time to pamper myself with a long, relaxing bath before I set about putting on makeup and styling my hair. I look through my closet and laugh as I stare at my office attire. None of it makes me feel like a woman, and I'm forced to dig deep into the back of my closet to find anything I feel sexy wearing.

My closet is a testament to how long I've been ignoring myself.

Donning a black cocktail dress that hugs my curves, I stare into the mirror. Running my hands over my body, I imagine the sensual touch of a stranger. Just thinking about it has my pussy growing wet.

As I gaze at my reflection, I feel increasingly like a lioness on the prowl for a lion strong enough to tame my raging sexual desire.

I take a cab, not wanting to deal with the hassle of a car, and tell the driver to take me to the Drake Hotel. The hotel is high-class and the perfect place for a discreet encounter. My excitement grows as we pull up to the grand entrance. Handing the driver a handsome tip, I step out of the vehicle, ready to conquer—and be conquered.

I can feel the gaze of every man on me as I make my way through the hotel foyer and leisurely head to the bar. I am in complete control as I sway my hips enticingly, inviting their lustful stares.

Sidling up to the bar counter, I take a seat and lay my clutch purse down. To my amusement, the bartender noticed me the moment I entered the bar and ignores his other patrons so that he can attend to me.

"What would you like to drink, pretty lady?" He then adds with a wink, "I know every drink in the book."

Wanting to make it a challenge for him, I tell him I'd like a Red Seal of Shimoda, curious to see if he can make the drink.

His eyes twinkle when he tells me, "You happen to be in luck, I have Suntory Toki Whisky in the back."

I nod to him, impressed.

While he mixes my drink, I scan the other men in the bar. Most seem to be here with colleagues, so I immediately dismiss them. But there are a few gentlemen who catch my eye, and one in particular who stands out from the rest.

He sits alone at a table, nursing a martini. When our eyes meet, I instantly feel a connection, but I quickly glance away. The game is not to appear overly eager. Eagerness equates to desperation, and I am not a desperate woman.

I have high standards that must be met. I want a man who is confident, but not arrogant. One who respects a successful woman but who is also not intimidated by her. Nothing is more disappointing than thinking you've found a lion only to have a puppy dog at your feet. I want to feed off his confidence in the bedroom and fully explore his desires as well as mine.

There are not many men who can meet my high standards, and I will not waste my time or share my body with anyone less.

My eyes drift over to him again. He's clean-cut but has an aura of mystery about him which intrigues me. Because he's piqued my curiosity, I give him a slight smile when I catch him staring again. The fire I see in his eyes leaves no doubt that we share a mutual attraction, but the question of whether or not we are compatible remains uncertain.

Another man enters the bar and takes a seat on the opposite side of the bar. I find his rough five-o'clock shadow and easy smile attractive. The man exudes an animal magnetism that is hard for me to resist. However, I've learned with experience that I need to be particularly careful with men like him. They can either be one of the best fucks I've ever had, or a complete disaster in bed.

It doesn't matter how attractive a man is, any man who concentrates on his own satisfaction over mine is a waste of my valuable energy.

A gentleman who is not on my radar buys me a drink and lifts his glass to me when the bartender tells me, "Compliments of the gentleman at the end of the bar" while sliding a margarita toward me.

I catch the man with the easy smile, who is sitting beside the guy, shaking his head in disgust. At least he understands...

Such a cliché gesture is lost on someone like me because I have zero interest in getting drunk tonight. I want to be sober when I decide who I am going to spend the night with. I quietly decline the drink and watch the disappointment on the guy's face as the bartender takes it away.

I refocus my attention on the man sitting at the table and stare longer than I should, purposely inviting his attention. I feel an inexplicable thrill as I slowly lift my glass and take a sip of my

Shimoda without breaking eye contact with him. I love the fact my red lipstick leaves an imprint on the glass that he can see.

Glancing at the man with the easy smile, I notice he is watching me with growing interest. He raises an eyebrow, a sexy smirk playing across his sensual lips.

Both men are worthy of my pursuit, but I can only choose one. Should I go with the man who has an air of mystery about him or the one with the animal magnetism?

Making up my mind, I finish my drink and pay the bartender. Picking up my clutch, I swing my hips alluringly so both men can admire my fine ass when I leave. Glancing back, I give the man sitting alone at the table a flirtatious smile before I head out the door.

Taking my time, I stop to take out my lipstick and reapply the rich red color before I slowly make my way to the elevators. I pause for a moment before pressing the button. As the elevator doors open, I hear a man clear his throat behind me.

Turning my head, I see my mystery man has responded to my invitation.

I nod and turn to him as the elevator doors close behind me.

"Would you be interested in dinner in my room?" he asks in a sultry voice.

"I would," I reply, taking the arm he offers.

Pressing the elevator button, he leads me into the elevator. Before the elevator doors close, I spot the man with the easy smile. He steps out of the bar and into the hallway, looking at me appreciatively.

There is an exhilarating thrill in knowing I am wanted by both men.

When the doors close, my mystery man faces me and looks deep into my eyes. "You could have any man in that room. Why did you choose me?"

I smile up at him with a playful glint in my eyes. "You look like someone who can be both gentle…and rough."

Pulling me to him, I can feel the strength of his growing erection pressed against my body. My nipples harden into tight buds in response to the intimate contact.

"I understand exactly what you need," he assures me as he leans in for a kiss. My breaths come in short gasps as he hesitates for a moment, hovering centimeters from my lips, just before he kisses me.

I moan with desire, my body melding against his as I lose myself in his fiery kisses. He runs his fingers through my hair, fisting it tightly while he ravages my mouth with his tongue.

My pussy drips with anticipation as I return his intoxicating kisses, our chemistry igniting as we connect to each other in the confined space.

The moment the elevator starts slowing down to stop at a floor, we break the embrace, turn away, and stare straight ahead while an older gentleman enters the elevator. He looks at us both, but his eyes linger on me as the doors close.

I wonder if he can feel the sexual tension in the air.

A small smile creeps across my lips as I stand there. I feel my mysterious lover taking my hand, out of the other passenger's view, and trailing his finger lightly across my sensitive palm. My pussy aches with pleasure, and I imagine his finger teasing my clit.

Lucky for us, three floors up, the man exits the elevator. I notice with satisfaction that there is a stiffness to the gentleman's gait.

God, how I love having that kind of power over men.

Once the doors close, I wrap my arms around the back of my handsome stranger's neck and begin kissing him with wild abandon. There is an undercurrent of vulnerability and trust in giving myself to a complete stranger. The element of the unknown fuels my lust and I bite his bottom lip.

He groans in response, grabbing my ass with his strong hands as he grinds his hard cock against me—

"Mama!" Hope cried out in desperation from within the house. Her voice was full of painful desperation.

Immediately dropping her journal, Brie rushed inside to find Hope standing in the middle of the room, sobbing for her.

"I'm right here, sweet pea. Mommy's right here," she said soothingly, wrapping Hope in her arms. The instant she touched her daughter, the tiny baby who was rescued from the compound came to Brie's mind, and tears filled her eyes.

That innocent child has no mother to comfort her.

Brie wiped her own tears away while crooning softly, "It's okay, my sweet little girl…"

It wasn't until hours later, after Brie put Hope down for her nap, that she remembered her journal. Hurrying outside to get it, she was horrified to find it was gone.

Rushing back inside, she asked Sir, "Did you see my journal, Sir? Please, please, tell me you did!"

Going to his office, Sir came back out, carrying it. "It is extremely important not to let this out of your sight, babygirl. You wouldn't want this journal getting in the hands of someone else."

She blushed, appalled by the thought. "I can't imagine anything worse!"

Thinking of Hope, she muttered, "Before I know it, our little munchkins will be reading. I'd better find a safer place for this journal."

"I wholeheartedly agree," he chuckled.

As she headed to the bedroom to find a secure place for it, Sir called after her, "I'm glad to see you're journaling again."

She turned to smile at him. "Me, too, Sir. It's been far too long."

Brie tucked her journal away on the top shelf in the back of their closet and smiled to herself, wondering if Sir had taken a peek at her newest entry.

Compassion

B rie woke with a start. Lying back on the pillow, she was overcome with a clear sense of urgency. Assuming it was the remnants of a dream, she attempted to go back to sleep. However, the moment she closed her eyes, a vision of Marquis Gray flashed in her mind. Following Sir's advice, she immediately concentrated on sending Marquis good thoughts and settled down to rest.

But as the day progressed, that sense of urgency returned and grew even stronger. Concerned, she went to speak to Sir about it. "I feel as if I should visit Marquis Gray. I know he said he doesn't want visitors, but I feel a need to see him, Sir."

Sir furrowed his brow. "An unexpected visit is not bound to go well, babygirl. The last thing I want is for you to be hurt, considering the current state he's in. There is a reason he's chosen to remain isolated."

"I know, Sir…" she agreed with sadness. "However, this pull on my heart is something I can't ignore."

Sir nodded thoughtfully and considered her request.

"If you feel you must go, then I support you. We can visit him tomorrow, after I finish work."

Shaking her head, Brie explained, "Sir, I feel like I need to go now—as in right this very minute."

"Unfortunately, I can't break away today."

After staring at Brie for several seconds, he finally sighed. "I've always advised you to trust your gut. That remains true now."

Holding out his arms to Brie, she rushed into them and he kissed her on the forehead. "If you are feeling that strongly about it, you must honor that impulse. I will inform Celestia that you are coming."

"Thank you, Sir!" she cried in relief, hugging him tightly.

Once she'd made the decision to go, she felt the tension ease up. Grabbing her purse, she gave him one last kiss.

But, as she was heading out the door, Sir called after her, "If things do not go well, leave before Gray has any chance of saying something you both will regret."

"Yes, Sir," she replied, feeling both anxious and resolute as she headed out the door.

When she arrived at their house, Brie was disgusted to see their home swarming with reporters. As soon as Brie hurried up to the house, Celestia opened the door before she had a chance to ring the doorbell.

"Please come in," she whispered, quickly ushering

Brie inside and shutting the door. Celestia's normally radiant face was marred with lines of worry and stress.

Brie immediately stopped to hug her. "It's going to be okay."

Tears came to the sweet woman's eyes. "I have never seen him like this. His soul is tortured and nothing I say or do has any effect. I'm at a loss at this point." Celestia's face crumbled into more tears when she confessed, "I feel like I'm losing him…"

Brie hugged her tighter, wanting to impart her strength onto Celestia. "You are his guiding light. He will not lose his way with you by his side. You must believe that."

She nodded, quickly wiping the tears from her face. "You're right. I cannot indulge in doubt. It does not honor my Master or my belief in God."

Brie hugged her again before turning to face the door to the study.

"Would you like me to go with you?" Celestia offered.

Brie let out a nervous sigh. "Thank you but no. I'll be okay."

"I'll start a pot of tea going, then. Sir Davis suggested the two of us should talk afterward."

Brie smiled at her, grateful for Sir's thoughtfulness. "That would be wonderful, Celestia."

Taking Brie's hands, she squeezed them in encouragement. "I'm so grateful you came, Brianna. I'll be on my knees, praying for you both."

Encouraged, Brie watched her head to the kitchen. And then, taking a deep breath, she walked up to the study door. Knocking once, she didn't wait for Marquis to respond before opening it and stepping inside.

Chills coursed through her body the moment she entered the room. The lights were off and the fire was out, leaving the room cold and dark in both temperature and ambiance. Brie rubbed her arms to stave off the sudden shiver she felt.

"Why are you here?" she heard Marquis Gray call out in the dark.

"I had to come, Asher."

"Why?" he demanded, his voice a force not to be denied.

Brie hesitated, challenged by the strength behind that voice. "I…I felt an urgent need to come that I could not deny."

She heard his startled intake of breath, and then the most terrifying sound she could imagine—his tortured sobs.

Brie made her way to him in the dark and knelt on the floor beside his chair. She was hesitant to touch Marquis because she did not have his permission, but the pain she felt radiating from him demanded a response.

Trusting her instincts, Brie bowed, pressing her forehead against his feet.

"Don't…" he choked out.

Even though she heard his command, she felt even more conviction when she kissed the leather of his shoes in an act of reverence and respect.

His grief-stricken cry broke the silence, shattering Brie's heart.

She remained still until she felt Marquis Gray's hand

on the back of her head.

"Look at me, pearl," he commanded in a hoarse voice.

Lifting her head up, she stared at him in the dim light filtering through the curtained windows.

His words gutted her when he spoke again. "I have been fighting against God. I am broken and can no longer be trusted…"

Marquis's voice was gruff with emotion when he confessed, "And then you come and bow at my feet in supplication." Reaching down, he grasped her chin, tilted her head up, and asked in a tortured voice, "Why would you do that?"

"I had to," she answered, her bottom lip trembling. "The urge was so strong, I couldn't ignore it."

"But to kiss my feet when I forbade it?"

Breathless with fear, she confessed, "I felt even more conviction in doing it."

Marquis let her chin go.

Sighing deeply, he slowly pushed himself up from his chair and went to start a fire. As the flames engulfed the wood in the fireplace, the light from it illuminated the room.

Once the fire was blazing, he returned to Brie and held out his hand to her. When Brie grasped it, he helped her to her feet and gestured for her to sit in the chair beside him.

Brie obediently sat down, keeping her gaze lowered.

"As you know, I have been facing a crisis of faith," Marquis stated in a low, pained voice. "I am questioning everything I know and believe and…I find myself lacking in both areas."

Brie glanced up, looking at him with sympathy. "I can't begin to imagine how painful that must be for a man with strong beliefs." When she finally met his gaze, she was confronted with the depths of his internal suffering and realized it was beyond anything in her limited experience.

Marquis said nothing, and the room fell into a heavy and uncomfortable silence.

Her heart racing, Brie shared what had been weighing heavily on her heart since their last conversation. "I understand that you feel culpable for the immense suffering Holloway caused me, Mary, and the others…but you're not."

She glanced down at her hands, fidgeting nervously. "I'm not wise like you, Asher. However, I've had a lot of time to think about it, and…" She took a deep breath, worried about how he would respond to her next words. "…Asher, I think it's foolish to blame yourself for being unable to discern Holloway's nature when he purposely avoided you for that very reason."

"Foolish?" he growled in irritation.

Bravely meeting the trainer's gaze, she stated with conviction, "You are not omniscient. Only God is…so, it all comes down to a matter of ego."

"*My* ego?" he snarled.

She nodded meekly.

Marquis narrowed his eyes. "You have no idea what I have done."

With her heart almost beating out of her chest, she pleaded, "Tell me."

He sat back in his chair, staring at her in silence.

"Please, Asher."

Her quiet pleas seemed to move him, and he shared in a calm voice cut with an undercurrent of bitterness as he spoke, "Very well, Mrs. Davis. I have already told you that Holloway flinched when I saw him at the prison. My wrath was so palpable that it had the power to pierce the glass between us and burrow straight into his black heart."

Marquis lowered his voice, "But what I didn't tell you was that he confided something to me during that encounter that involved you."

His tone led Brie to believe it was something unspeakably perverse. Although she was terrified, she asked in a fearful whisper, "What did he say?"

Marquis paused for several seconds before honoring her request. "Holloway told me that he wanted to send Sir Davis and me a message when he kidnapped you." Brie could tell by the change in Marquis's voice—the softness of it—that it pained him to say it out loud. "He left your collar on because he wanted us to find your body broken and unrecognizable except for the collar around your neck."

Brie closed her eyes, whimpering in horror.

He added, "...to emphasize that we had been unable to protect you."

Marquis's voice suddenly rose in temper and volume. "It felt as if the wrath of God was speaking through me when I told that bastard there was no escape from what he had done."

Snorting in gratification, he shared, "It was then that

I saw the fear of God in those soulless eyes of his."

Brie silently cheered, experiencing a sense of justice knowing that the monster had been afraid before his death.

Marquis narrowed his eyes, confessing, "I was not satisfied by simply seeing his fear, however. When he claimed that God would forgive him despite the evil he'd done, I was determined to extinguish any hope he'd been clinging to. I told him that God forgives sinners, but there is no forgiveness for an unrepentant heart. That his pleas of mercy would never be heard. Before I left, I proclaimed that retribution was coming for him."

Marquis looked at Brie, his eyes growing darker. "Do you want to know the last words I spoke to him?"

Swallowing hard, she nodded.

"There are far worse things than death…"

Goosebumps rose on Brie's skin when she heard his final proclamation.

Marquis looked away. "Although they found no evidence I was involved, the authorities brought me in for questioning because Holloway was found dead within an hour after returning to his cell. But even knowing he's dead, I still burn with unbearable rage."

Brie reached out to touch his hand.

He instinctively pulled away, looking at her sadly.

"You could not know this, pearl, but I woke up this morning consumed by this rage that I cannot control. Knowing how dark and perverted my soul had become in the wake of what happened, I have separated myself from the Lord and those around me. But today, I was desperate to end the torment and cried out to God, commanding Him to strike me dead as proof of His existence."

Marquis closed his eyes, his voice breaking when he told her, "Lightening failed to strike, but then you walked into the study uninvited and knelt at my feet. Instead of the condemnation I rightfully deserved, you showed me compassion."

He opened his eyes, staring deep into hers. "Now that I have my answer, I know what I must do."

The Girls

B rie drove back home, quietly contemplating what had happened.

After Marquis Gray's declaration about having his answer, he had followed Brie out of the study and then gone directly to Celestia.

The moment she heard him walk into the kitchen, Celestia stopped reciting her prayers mid-sentence and broke into tears.

Helping her to her feet, Marquis commanded gently, "No more tears need fall." Drying her eyes with his handkerchief, he'd then taken her by the hand and led her out of the kitchen, leaving Brie standing there alone. Not wanting to interrupt their private time together, she simply left and headed back home.

On her return, she went to Sir's office and detailed what happened. However, she chose not to mention what Marquis shared with her about Holloway's decision to leave her collar on during her captivity. It was too horrifying to repeat—and she worried about Sir's reaction to it.

Seeing how it tormented Marquis, Brie could not bear for Sir to suffer any more than he already had. Although she'd promised to never keep anything from him, this was an act of mercy on her part. There was nothing good that would come from him knowing about Holloway's plans. Such a dark secret deserved to be buried along with his dead corpse.

Surprised to hear of her actions during the visit, Sir asked her, "What drove you to bow and kiss his feet?"

Brie frowned as she thought back on it. "I really don't know, Sir."

"Interesting…"

"It was a little frightening, actually," she confessed. "Especially since it was Marquis. But you encouraged me to trust my gut, and I did." Suddenly concerned, she asked, "Do you think I shouldn't have, Sir?"

"Although it was an odd thing to do, it appears to have had a positive result." He smiled at her tenderly, addressing her unspoken concern, "I do not question your decision, babygirl."

She leaned forward to give him a kiss. "I'm grateful because my heart's desire is to always please you, Master."

He grasped the back of her neck and kissed her deeply, murmuring, "Ever my good submissive…"

Brie knew that before long, she would have no time to

spare. Now that she was working on the documentary again, it would cut deeply into her life. Before her schedule got too crazy, she decided to ask Lea and Mary to spend an afternoon hanging together.

Originally, Brie toyed with the idea of returning to the old bar near the Training Center. She thought maybe they could meet there for old times' sake, but then she quickly nixed that idea. It would only end in disaster, with scores of reporters in a frenzy to discover who was responsible for Holloway's untimely death.

Not wanting to take a chance to meet in public and invite that kind of unwanted attention, Brie asked them to come to her place. As an extra precaution, Sir suggested she also enlist some of Rytsar's men to guard the perimeters in case any reporter tried to harass the threesome while they were relaxing on the beach.

It was important to Brie that she kept close ties with her friends right now, especially Mary. It would be easy to get lost in the daily pressures and responsibilities of life and lose touch with one another.

Sir had set up three loungers for them, and Brie had a cooler full of drinks and snacks so they could spend the entire afternoon chilling on the beach without interruption.

Lea was the first to join her on the beach. She waltzed up to Brie with the confidence of a woman in love with her life. Brie noted that she was dressed in a pink bikini that showed off her impressive boobs—and also happened to match the color of the diamond on her collar.

The first thing Brie did was tackle her with a hug.

"Look at you, all glam with that fancy collar around your neck."

She played with it, grinning at Brie. "You know, I love it so dang much that I have the urge to strip right here so it's the only thing I'm wearing—just so I can properly show it off."

"Please don't," Mary retorted, walking up behind her. Before Lea could react, Mary whipped her towel, snapping Lea on the butt.

Lea let out a yelp and cried, "Not fair!"

Mary just snorted, laid her towel out on one of the loungers, and plunked herself down.

"Nice to see you, too," Brie stated sarcastically, shaking her head at Mary's flippancy.

Mary glanced up at them both and shrugged. "I only came to get a tan, what can I say?"

Lea twisted around to look at the red mark on her shapely ass. She rubbed her butt, trying to soothe the bruised skin. Brie noticed several surfers rubbernecking as they walked past. Lea was oblivious, complaining to Mary, "That hurt!"

Mary folded her arms, snorting in amusement. "That reminds me of a joke…"

Both Brie and Lea shot surprised glances at each other.

When they failed to respond, Mary looked up at them from the lounger. "What? You don't want to hear it?"

"Sure?" Lea said hesitantly, still rubbing her butt.

"So, this chesty blonde goes to the doctor and complains that her ass hurts. When the doctor asks where, she tells him it hurts right around the entrance."

Smirking, Mary delivered her punchline. "The doctor chuckles, telling her, 'Yeah, well that's the exit, young lady. As long as you treat it like an entrance, it'll probably keep hurting.'"

Brie chuckled. "Speaking from experience, it feels sooo good!"

Lea gave her a high-five. "You got that right, girl-friend."

Laying her towel down, Lea settled down beside Mary and stroked her collar. "So, what do you think?"

Mary glanced at it with disinterest. "Looks like a yoke to me, but at least it's pretty. I will say, the ceremony was first-rate, and you rocked that dress. Your man has good taste."

Brie looked at Mary in confusion. "Wait, you saw the ceremony?"

"Watched the whole damn thing."

Lea patted Mary's arm patiently. "Yeah, even though she's a pain in the ass—like literally—I would never leave Mary Quite Contrary out of something so important. We're the three musketeers after all!" Looking at Brie, she explained, "I asked the photographer to set up a camera so Mary could watch the ceremony live."

Brie was touched knowing Mary had been able to share that special moment. It spoke to how strong their bonds had become.

Lea added, "Even though Mary has given me endless crap about getting collared, I know deep down, she's really happy for us."

Mary snorted. "The only thought I had as I watched

you get down on your knees and offer your collar was, 'Damn, another one bites the dust…' She tsked. "I thought you were smarter than that, Lea the Lame, but you had to prove me wrong."

Lea lay back in her lounger, grinning. "If I'm wrong, then this girl doesn't ever want to be right."

"Go ahead, keep telling yourself that," Mary snickered.

After Brie grabbed a drink for everyone, she moved to the spot beside Mary. Taking a long, quenching sip, she lay back and smiled up at the sky. "I love being here with you two."

"And I love the free drinks," Mary said, holding up her glass.

Lea sighed contentedly. "I couldn't be happier…" Turning to Mary, she added with a sly smile, "I've noticed you and Faelan hanging around a lot more these days. Is something going on between you two?"

Mary choked on her drink. "Hell no! That ship sailed ages ago." She paused for a moment, then let out a deep sigh. "I knew the moment I threw his collar in the trash that it would crush his heart."

Looking at the two of them, she smiled sadly. "Even though I didn't realize it then, I'm glad that I was a selfish, greedy whore back then. If I hadn't been, Faelan would be dead right now."

Brie frowned. "What do you mean?"

"Greg had his sights set on me, Stinks. If Faelan had gotten in the way, I have no doubt he would have 'disappeared'." Mary visibly shuddered. "I can't imagine the terrible things that monster would have done to

Faelan before he offed him."

Overcome with profound sadness, Brie told her, "I hate that he came in between the two of you."

Mary laughed. "Don't be a twit. I never would have stayed with Faelan. It was nice for a while, but I can't stand being tied down like that."

"Even with someone who loved you for who you are, warts and all?" Lea asked her, sounding confused by Mary's declaration.

Mary rolled her eyes. "He was a fucking idiot to get mixed up with me. He knew it. I knew it. But…" She shrugged. "…it was fun while it lasted."

"So, you're saying Holloway wasn't the reason you broke it off? It had everything to do with you?" Brie asked her.

"Yeah. I can't stand a guy getting too close. It seriously creeps me out. But now, since there's no chance of the two of us getting back together, it's nice. We can just be friends with none of those creepy strings attached. I like it much better this way."

Brie braved bringing up the heated topic again. "Mary, I still think you need to find your birth father."

"Shut the fuck up, bitch!" Mary snarled.

Brie looked at her compassionately. "Maybe if you can reconcile your relationship with your birth father, you will finally be able to love yourself."

"Oh, my God, Stinks! Don't start shoving that self-love crap at me now."

Brie persisted. "Don't you get it? You couldn't allow Faelan to love you because you don't love yourself."

Lea let out a gasp. "You're right, Brie!"

Mary narrowed her eyes, looking like she was about to explode. "You don't know shit about me. Neither of you do." She let out a low growl and grumbled, "Fuck, if I'd known you two were going to gang up on me today, I never would have come. No tan is worth this."

Brie and Lea looked at each other in concern. They'd been friends long enough to weather Mary's outbursts because they both knew it came from a place of deep pain.

"Don't you dare say another word about it," Mary warned, gulping down the rest of her drink.

"Gotcha," Brie agreed, choosing to respect her demand. But she silently hoped Mary would mull over her words later, when she was alone.

Trying to lighten the mood, Lea suggested, "Why don't we go for a swim, you two?"

"Feel free to go drown yourself if you want. I'm not moving from this spot," Mary declared.

Worried that something more was going on, Brie asked nonchalantly, "Would anyone like another drink?"

"Thought you would never ask," Mary snapped.

After handing out another round, Brie settled down in her lounger and glanced at Lea in concern.

"So, Brie, how are your parents doing?" Lea asked, trying to redirect the conversation.

Brie laughed uncomfortably. "Umm…things have been a little tense, actually. My dad kind of lost it and said something he shouldn't have to Sir. I'm still trying to forgive him."

"How did Sir react?" Lea asked.

"He was a gentleman and handled it far more kindly

than my father deserved."

Lea smiled encouragingly. "At least you didn't have both men yelling at each other."

"True. But it's hard, you guys. I know my father loves me, but ever since I was rescued, things have been weird between us." She sighed heavily. "I think he still blames Sir for what happened with Holloway because he introduced me to the lifestyle. It's like all the progress we made got wiped away."

"That's rough, girlfriend," Lea with sympathy.

Mary rolled over onto her stomach, cradling her head in her folded arms. "I think you should reconcile your relationship with your birth father."

Brie snorted, amused Mary was spitting back her own advice. "Ha-ha…"

"She's right, you know," Lea agreed.

"I don't see how I can," Brie confessed to them. "Sir has gone to extraordinary lengths to help me heal, but my dad just can't let go of his belief that Sir is ultimately to blame. It's infuriating to me!"

Lea looked at her with sympathy. "I hate to say it, but you're going to have to talk it out. It would be a shame for you to lose your parents over this, and then there's your children to think about."

Brie let out a painful sigh, knowing it was unfair to her children. "Although you're right, I just don't want to deal with it right now."

Lea squeezed her hand. "No need to force it, girl-friend. Wait until you're ready."

The three lay in silence for a long time. Thankfully, the relaxing sounds of the waves brought a sense of peace that seemed to slowly eat away at the tension between them.

"Mind getting us another round of drinks, Stinks?"

Brie got up from the lounger as Lea's infectious laughter filled the air.

"Oh, I like how that rhymes—drinks, stinks…" she giggled.

Mary looked at her tiresomely. "Amazing how the simplest things amuse you."

Lea shrugged. "I just look at life differently."

Mary huffed. "You got that right."

"So, what's been going on with you?" Brie asked Mary after she returned with a new round of drinks and settled back down.

The moment Brie heard Mary's troubled sigh, it suddenly made sense why she'd been so surly all afternoon. Something was seriously wrong.

"What's happened?" Brie prodded.

Mary just shook her head and took another sip of her drink.

"Spit it out or I'll make a joke, and you know I've got thousands of them," Lea threatened.

Rolling her eyes, Mary looked up at the sky. "Greg's lawyers met with me last week."

Brie sat up in alarm. "What the hell did they want from you?"

Mary's face twisted in pain, and it looked as if she was about to retch. "Apparently, Greg had a God complex, because the fucker never made a will. Due to his error in judgment, I'm stuck getting a portion of his inheritance." She shook her head violently. "But I don't want any of it—not one penny."

"How is that even possible?" Brie asked. "You were never married, and I heard California doesn't recognize common-law marriages."

Mary frowned when she repeated what the lawyers told her. "They droned on about joint checking accounts, credit cards, plus some property I had no clue about. Since we lived together acting as 'mutual companions'—whatever the fuck that means—it somehow qualifies as a stable, marriage-like relationship in the eyes of the California courts." Mary snorted in disgust. "The fucking irony is that Greg insisted on making everything joint because he wanted control over my income and every fucking penny I spent."

"Talk about irony," Lea muttered.

"I don't want his fucking blood money!" Mary howled in rage.

A couple walking along the shore stopped to stare at her. One of Rytsar's men quickly walked up to the couple and hurried them along.

Brie was puzzled. "I don't get it. Holloway was an intelligent person. Knowing how he felt about you, why wouldn't he have protected his assets when he knew California law? It makes no sense to me."

Lea shook her head, equally perplexed.

"Oh, my God!" Mary suddenly cried, her face draining of all color. "Greg never considered it an issue because he expected to outlive me."

What Mary said next caused goosebumps to rise on Brie's skin.

"That bastard planned to kill me all along!"

Lying back in her chair, Mary stared up at the sky, her face pale and full of shock.

Brie lay there in stunned silence, the reality of what Holloway planned to do hovering over her like a suffocating cloud.

The silence was finally broken when Mary whimpered to herself, "Why can't I ever be free of him...?"

Good Thoughts

With Master Nosh's interview set to be filmed in a week, Brie decided to call Tono and share the happy news with him. He had always been a big supporter of her work, and she knew he would enjoy hearing about the new developments regarding her documentary.

Tono immediately picked up when she dialed his number. "I thought you might be calling."

"Why is that, Tono?" she laughed, her soul instantly responding to the soothing sound of his voice.

"I was just thinking about you."

She grinned. "I love that our connection remains strong despite the distance between us."

"It brings me comfort as well," he agreed, his voice tender. "It is good to hear your voice."

"I was thinking the same thing, Tono. Your voice has a calming effect I can't explain."

"I'm glad to hear it. How are you…really?"

Her smile grew wider when she told him, "I'm well. Better than I'd hoped."

"That *is* welcomed news."

"That's actually the reason I called. I feel well enough that I've started working on the documentary again. I am even filming an extra interview for it."

She swore she could hear the smile in his voice when Tono said, "I cannot tell you how happy that makes me to hear that. Who are you interviewing?"

Brie let out a happy sigh, hardly able to contain her excitement when she told him, "Master Nosh, the head trainer of the Dominant course."

"Ah…" Tono said, sounding pleased. "I know the man well."

"You do?"

"Yes, Master Nosh asked me to demonstrate Kinbaku to his students in the course."

She was shocked by the news and exclaimed, "I never knew that!"

"I did it for many years but, by the time you and I met, I had moved on to other things."

Brie shook her head, laughing. "Wouldn't it have been funny if you'd been demonstrating when Sir attended the course?"

"I did."

"What!" she cried again. "How come you never mentioned it to me before?"

"I suppose it never came up," he chuckled. "I'm not a man who lives in the past."

Brie shook her head, her mind completely blown. "It appears Sir must think the same way since this is the first I've ever heard of it."

Tono laughed. "Would it have changed anything if

you had known?"

Snorting in amusement, she admitted, "I suppose not."

A companionable silence settled in between them. Out of curiosity, she asked, "What was Sir like back then?"

"Determined—just as he is now."

She giggled. "Somehow, I'm not surprised."

"I anticipate good things will come from your interview with Master Nosh," Tono told her. "He is a remarkable man."

"I completely agree. Although, I have to admit I find him a bit intimidating."

He chuckled. "His wife is a perfect balance to his imposing countenance."

"You know Nenove as well?" she asked in surprise.

"I do. They were kind enough to let me stay with them for six months after I came to the United States. It gave me enough time to save up money to live on my own."

"Tono!" Brie cried in disbelief. "I feel like I don't even know who you are."

"You know me," he stated in a serious tone.

Brie held back any further protests because he was right. They knew each other on a much deeper level. What had happened in his past didn't matter, other than how it had shaped him into the person he was now. "You're right, Tono. I know you."

Still…she could just imagine how adorable it would be to see Tono and Sir together at that age and asked him, "You wouldn't happen to have any pictures of you and Sir together, would you?"

"Why?" He snorted in amusement. "Do you need proof?"

"No, of course not," she giggled. "I would just love to see what the two of you looked like back then."

"I'm certain I have photos of Sir Davis in storage. I will look through my files when we're finished touring."

"So, enough about me," Brie insisted. "How are you doing, Tono?"

"Autumn and I are having an exceptionally successful tour. Many of our venues are sold out."

"That's exciting!"

"Autumn has a dedicated following now."

Brie chuckled. "I can't believe it when I think of the shy girl I met who refused to uncover her face... You performed a miracle."

"No," he insisted. "I simply unveiled what has always been there. She is the personification of courage and graceful strength. Autumn is truly a sight to behold on the stage.

"So, will we be seeing you guys again soon?" Brie asked hopefully.

"I had originally expected to return in two months, but we've been asked to extend our tour."

Brie frowned and cautioned him, "Don't overextend yourself. You are still recovering from that virus. I worry about you."

"There's no reason to worry," he assured her.

Brie heard Autumn call out in the background, "Tono, is that Brie?"

"It is, kohana. Would you like to speak with her?"

"I would love to!"

Speaking to Brie, Tono said, "I will speak with you again after you two are finished."

Autumn sounded concerned when she asked, "How are you doing, Brie? We never stop thinking about you."

"I'm actually doing well enough that I have started working on the documentary again."

"I'm so relieved to hear that. The horror of your captivity hasn't been far from my mind."

Knowing it wasn't only Tono she was indebted to, Brie said, "I want to thank you for caring for Tono after Holloway captured me."

"I was terrified for you and Tono! I still remember the day you were kidnapped because Tono had been uneasy for hours before Sir Davis even called. The moment he got off the phone, he laid out his jute mat and sat down to meditate. When he didn't speak or move from that spot the entire day, I started bringing him water and food."

Her voice caught when she shared, "Brie, I have never seen Tono like that before. There were many times I walked in to find him silently crying."

Brie felt heartsick when she heard how much Tono had suffered on her behalf.

"The day you were rescued…"

Brie heard the fear in her voice. "What, Autumn?"

"He let out a scream that rocked me to the core. It was such a terrifying sound that I still can't get it out of my mind."

"I had no idea…" Brie muttered, her heart beating frantically at the news.

Quickly changing the tone of the conversation, Autumn told her, "I can't begin to tell you how thankful I am that you not only survived but are thriving again."

Brie instantly thought about the pillow Master Anderson had given her with the word THRIVE stitched onto it. It was amazing to think that after being almost shattered, she'd found a way back from the darkness because of all the people who helped her to reach this point.

"I am thriving, Autumn," she agreed. "And from what Tono said, you are, too."

She gushed with excitement, "I am having so much fun on this tour, and I'm getting to meet so many new people who support our work. I can't believe this is my life now. I know I've said before how much I love to travel. But it's more than that, Brie. I feed off the energy of the audience. There is no bigger high than when I'm flying in the air, bound in rope, receiving all their energy."

"I can't imagine it, but it sounds incredible."

"It truly is!" she declared joyfully. "I'd better let you go, because I've got to pack for the next leg of the tour. But I'm so happy to hear you are doing better!"

"And I'm thrilled for you, Autumn." Knowing that she was every bit the jokester that Lea was, Brie asked, "Do you have a joke for me before you go?"

Autumn chuckled. "I don't do that anymore."

"Oh?"

"Now that I have this new life, I've let go of childish things."

It struck Brie as a little sad. "Well, I wish you continued success on the tour."

"Thank you! And I am wishing you continued healing, my friend."

Handing the phone back to Tono, she called out to Brie, "Bye…!"

"It is truly a gift to know that you are doing well," Tono confessed to Brie.

She caught a hint of sorrow in his voice and immediately asked, "What's wrong, Tono? I sensed something was wrong when you visited me, and I hear it in your voice now."

When she heard his uncomfortable sigh, she insisted, "There's no point in keeping it from me. I'm doing well now, and it will only drive me crazy if you don't tell me."

He chuckled sadly. "Yes, I know you."

"Then please tell me…"

He said nothing for several moments, forcing Brie to wait patiently for his answer.

"It has to do with my mother."

Brie frowned. "What is she demanding now?"

"She's dying, Brie."

Knowing how complicated their relationship was, she asked Tono, "How does that make you feel?"

"Lost."

The pain in his voice hurt her heart, and she immediately begged, "What can I do?"

"There is nothing to be done. My mother has an inoperable brain tumor." He groaned painfully. "This has put me in a difficult position, and not one I am certain I can navigate."

Clutching the phone, she asked, "How do you

mean?"

"On the practical side, I cannot attend to her unless we cancel the remaining tour. Having done it once when my father fell ill, it could put future tours in jeopardy, and I will take a hard hit financially. On an emotional level, I'm unsure if I would be able to take on that responsibly without causing myself harm because of our caustic relationship. And I am *certain* Autumn would wither under the weight of her constant criticism."

He sighed heavily. "There are many things that remain unresolved between my mother and me. If I am being honest…I would like meaningful closure with the woman."

"That's understandable, Tono. You deserve that opportunity."

"Regrettably, because of the nature of her tumor, the window for that opportunity is closing. The doctor warned me that as it grows, she will experience changes in her mood, personality, and way of thinking."

"Oh, Tono! I'm sorry this is happening to you—and to her."

"As am I," he answered gravely.

"Is there anything I can do for you?" Brie pleaded, needing a way to help him.

"Concentrate on your documentary. It will bring me happiness to know that you are pouring your time and heart into something you are passionate about."

Brie let out a small sob. "My heart is breaking for you."

"It's important that you devote your energy to the things you can control. I do not need or want you to expend it on concern for me. This journey, whether I want it or not, is one I must accept."

Brie closed her eyes, desperate to bring peace to his soul. "I promise to send you good thoughts every time I think of you."

"I will receive them with gratitude, toriko."

"When I film the interview with Master Nosh next week, I will be wearing the orchid in my hair so you can be there with me in spirit."

She heard the affection in his voice when he said, "Please give Master Nosh my best when you see him."

"I will."

Before hanging up, Tono told her, "In uncertain times, knowing those you care about are well brings an abundance of peace."

Brie sat there afterward, her heart aching for Tono. Keeping her promise to him, she immediately closed her eyes.

I'm sending you my love and good thoughts, Tono.

Master Nosh

B rie was in her upstairs office, busy writing her finalized plan for the interview with Master Nosh the following day, when her text notification went off on her phone. She glanced over at her children playing on the floor beside her desk as she picked it up. The moment she read the text, Brie let out a squeal of joy:

Radost moya, have you missed your Russian?

Rather than text him back, she immediately dialed his number. As soon as he picked up, she blurted, "I've missed you more than you know! I've been worried after not hearing from you for so long."

He chuckled. "Siberia is a big place. Bigger than your puny country."

She laughed. "Well, you know, size doesn't matter…"

"Ha!"

Just hearing his voice caused Brie to grip the phone tightly, her cheeks hurting from smiling so hard.

180

His voice warm, Rytsar told her, "I see from your last text that you finally opened my gift from the ranch."

"I did, and I'm deeply touched by your thoughtfulness. I have Wildflower's photo sitting on my nightstand. Whenever I look at that beautiful horse, I feel like I'm getting a giant hug from you."

"That pleases me," he stated in satisfaction. "You will be happy to know I am finalizing the transfer of the creature right now."

Her jaw dropped. "You finally caught Lilly?"

"I did," he answered, grunting in satisfaction. "I am transporting her to the facility myself. Unfortunately, that does mean I will soon be out of range again, but I didn't want you to worry needlessly."

She let out a huge breath of relief, the sound resonating deep in her soul. Brie hadn't allowed herself to think of the consequences of Lilly's escape. She'd simply been too raw emotionally. But hearing Rytsar's news that there was no longer a threat had her feeling positively lightheaded.

"It feels…" Brie paused for a moment, searching for the right words. "…like I can finally breathe again."

"That is what I have been fighting for, *radost moya*," he said, his voice hoarse and impassioned.

"That must mean your plan worked!"

"It did," he stated proudly.

"How did you end up capturing her?"

"I will tell you soon enough."

"Oh, my goodness, does that mean you're returning to the States?" she asked hopefully.

"Soon enough," he repeated. "I must wait until Dr.

Volkov is finished conducting a series of psychological tests to assess her current needs. While he concentrates on that, I will be testing the security of the facility with the creature locked inside." He chuckled wickedly. "It is a task I am particularly looking forward to…"

Brie cautioned him, "Please don't take any unnecessary risks with her."

Rytsar snorted. "Do not worry. I have everything under control now."

Brie heard Titov call his name in the background.

"It must be goodbye for now, *radost moya*. Take heart. I go to fortify a future for you and the babes. Give them a kiss from their *dyadya*."

After ending the call, Brie sat there in stunned silence, staring at the computer screen. Rytsar had done exactly what he'd promised.

She looked at her two children, a state of pleasant shock washing over her.

The next day, Brie arrived at the Training Center an hour early. She wanted to give herself enough time to set up the camera and lighting for Master Nosh's interview. Knowing his tight schedule for the day, she planned to make the most of their time together.

Brie gathered the equipment out of her car and headed directly to the front desk. She called out to Rachael as she walked up, "Hello, Miss Dunningham!"

Rachael looked up from her computer and smiled.

"Mrs. Davis, what a pleasure to see you again."

"I can't believe I'm really here, filming again," she said, setting down her equipment for a moment. "It feels so much like old times that I need someone to pinch me just to prove this is real."

"I must say, you are positively glowing today," Rachael complimented. "Is there anything I can do to help?"

"Just let Master Nosh know I've arrived and tell him I'm looking forward to our interview in an hour."

"It will be my pleasure, Mrs. Davis."

As Brie was picking up her equipment, she heard a familiar voice behind her say, "Let me help you with that, darlin'."

Brie turned and smile at Master Anderson. "This is a fun surprise, thank you!"

He grinned as he grabbed her things and headed toward the elevators. "I was pleased to hear you were coming tonight to film with Master Nosh."

She looked up at him, beaming. "I'm more excited than I can say!"

He chuckled warmly as they stepped into the elevator. "It's good to see you thriving, young Brie."

She nodded, grateful to Master Anderson for his part in her recovery. "So, how have the wedding plans been going?"

He laughed. "Shey wants something simple to keep costs low, but I want something grand and extravagant."

Brie giggled. "Poor girl has no idea she's marrying into money."

He smirked. "No, she doesn't. And it's making this

whole wedding thing a humorous challenge for me."

Stepping out of the elevator, Master Anderson led her down a long hallway and stopped at one of the classroom doors. "As Headmaster of the Center, I assigned this room for you tonight."

He winked at her as she opened the door. Brie entered the room, thrilled by how large it was. "Thank you, Master Anderson!"

Placing her equipment on a table, he told her, "I'd wish you good luck, but I know you won't need it. Knock it out of the park, young Brie."

"I plan to," she grinned, touched by his belief in her.

The moment he left, Brie called her assistant Levi, who was joining her for the shoot. "Hey Levi, it looks like I'm going to need you to bring extra lighting and another microphone."

Brie was grateful to have an assistant on this shoot. After a lengthy discussion with Michael Schmidt, she'd decided to film the interview using her original camera so it would blend seamlessly in with the other interviews she'd filmed.

Setting up her camera in the corner for the interview, Brie arranged the light reflectors and adjusted them several times before she was satisfied. Glancing down at her watch, she noted the time and got out her list of questions.

Brie was especially eager to film the BDSM scene Master Nosh would be demonstrating. She had never seen fire flogging before and was curious to see what it was like. The idea of it thrilled her, and she was honored that she would be the first to film it for a worldwide audience.

Levi promptly arrived and set up for the demonstration so that Brie would be able to transition from the interview to the demonstration with little loss of time. Tonight, she wanted everything to be as seamless and professional as she could make it for Master Nosh.

As she read over her list of questions one final time, she was pleased to find she was not nearly as anxious as she thought she would be. Playing with the white orchid in her hair, Brie thought of Tono and smiled.

I feel your presence, Tono.

The moment Master Nosh arrived, Brie asked him to sit down so she could make adjustments with her camera before they began. While she did, she told Master Nosh, "Ren Nosaka wanted me to give you his best."

The trainer smiled at the mention of his name. "Ren…I haven't seen him around for some time now."

"He's been on a world tour," Brie explained. "It's become so successful that he's being asked to extend the tour."

"I'm not surprised," Master Nosh stated. "Even at eighteen, he was an incomparable talent."

Brie stopped what she was doing and told him, "I recently learned that he used to do demonstrations for the Dominant Training course."

Master Nosh looked directly at the lens of the camera when he told her, "Ren has the rare ability to be exceptionally skilled at his profession, and yet, he has the insight and patience to teach even the most inexperienced novice."

She smiled, remembering how infinitely patient Tono

had been with her more recently. Following her trauma, he'd spent hours reintroducing her to the love of jute...

It was extremely hard for Brie not to pepper Master Nosh with more questions about Tono. But, knowing time was short, she hit record and sat down. "First, I want to tell you how much I appreciate you taking the time to let me interview you today."

"Certainly," he answered, staring at her intently.

Starting with the first question on her list, she asked, "Many people are familiar with the Submissive Training Center but have never heard of the Dominant Training course offered at the Center. Can you tell me more about the course?"

He nodded. "We seek to expand the minds of the Dominants who attend our course. Our students are not just instructed on a wide variety of skill sets found in BDSM. We also dissect what it means to be a Dominant, and walk each student through the process of defining their path as a successful Dominant. Our graduates are not only well-versed in tools and techniques but are also well rounded in their communication and leadership skills as a Dominant."

Brie smiled knowingly. "As a submissive, I am fortunate to have been collared by one of the Center's leading graduates. I'm curious, Master Nosh. How is an applicant selected for the Dominant course from the multitude of entries the Center receives?"

He cleared his throat thoughtfully. "We have a rigorous application process in place. The program here at the Training Center allows us to devote our time and resources to those individuals who are motivated to succeed and still humble enough to learn." He looked directly at the camera lens when he added, "People with inflated egos need not apply."

Brie appreciated his succinct answers about the Center and was interested in seeing how he would respond to her next question. "How did you come to choose the BDSM lifestyle, Master Nosh?"

He leaned forward in his chair. "It came naturally to me. As a young man, I had a thirst for expanding my knowledge and exploring my own limitations. When I was accepted to Dartmouth College, my college peers introduced me to the BDSM lifestyle. I found the power exchange dynamic between a Dominant and their submissive fascinating and explored it extensively while I was there. After graduating, I returned to the reservation and had the great fortune to have my interests align with a partner who had an equal level of curiosity and the same desire to explore such a dynamic within the same cultural framework."

Brie noticed that Master Nosh chose not to mention Nenove by name and made a mental note not to inadvertently say it during the interview. "What made you choose to leave the Cheyenne reservation to pursue a career as head trainer of the Dominant course?"

He gazed at Brie for a moment before answering. "After embracing the BDSM lifestyle, I found a high level of satisfaction in both my personal and professional life. As a result, I sought to share that discovery with others. Knowing the exceptional reputation of the Submissive Training Center, I approached them to offer my insight and service for Dominant Training."

Brie found that exceedingly fascinating and followed up with another question. "What insight do you feel you bring to the training, Master Nosh?"

Master Nosh leaned forward, his eyes magnetic. "Most people are unaware of it, but there is a natural frequency and rhythm to every living thing on this planet. Every person has the ability to tap into it. I first encountered it while performing the Sun Dance ritual. I later found there was the potential to tap into my partner's natural frequency during a well-executed BDSM scene."

Brie had once read that during the Sun Dance ritual, some individuals had bone skewers inserted through a small fold of the skin on their upper chest, which was then connected to a pole by a leather thong. These individuals offered up their sacrifices to fulfill personal vows, and many experienced a trance-like state.

Master Nosh asked her, "What is more powerful between two people than connecting on that frequency?"

Brie nodded, remembering her recent conversation with Sir when she had confessed, *It's as if we're on the same frequency, and the resonance it creates is powerful.* She smiled at the head trainer. "That is an interesting perspective."

"Life is about perspective and mindfulness, wouldn't you agree? Once we understand that we are all one with the Earth and everything in it, we can embrace our place in this world and help it to thrive."

Brie looked at him, unable to hide her smile of understanding as she processed his statement. After several seconds, she noticed her assistant Levi motioning her to continue with her questions.

"I agree, Master Nosh," she answered, glancing down at her notes to find her place. Scanning them, she looked up and asked, "Do you have a tool that you prefer to use during a BDSM scene?"

The head trainer smiled enticingly when he answered, "Would you like me to show it to you?"

"Absolutely."

Master Nosh reached down and picked up his tool bag. Unzipping it, he produced two floggers. The tails were made of an unusual-looking yellow rope. Brie hadn't seen anything like them before.

Holding one up, he explained, "These floggers are made of Kevlar rope and are fire-resistant."

Brie couldn't hide her excitement when she asked, "Would you be willing to give us a demonstration?"

His eyes lit up when he answered, "Of course."

Dancing Flames

B efore Master Nosh began the scene, he lit a bundle of white sage and moved to different points in the room, thin wisps of smoke trailing after him while the air filled with a soothing, minty-earthy scent.

After a few minutes, the bundle naturally burned out and he placed it reverently on a large abalone shell he had set out. He then called out a command and Nenove, along with two other submissives, entered the room.

One, the spotter, was assigned to watch over the scene and stood armed with a wet cloth to protect Nenove from any stray flames that might escape. The other submissive held a hand drum. She knelt on the floor, waiting for Master Nosh's command. When he gave it, she began to play a steady, driving beat.

Master Nosh held out his hand to Nenove. She immediately joined him, her head bowed in reverence to her Master. She wore a simple leather corset and a deerskin skirt that sat low on her hips. She sported a decorative head wrap that had been soaked in water, and

Brie noted that it completely covered her hair.

Using his strong hands, Master Nosh positioned her body so she was facing a tall bench she could lean against for support. He then took his time unlacing her corset. Master Nosh handed it to the other submissive, exposing Nenove's bare back to the camera.

Master Nosh moved back a few paces to check if Nenove was positioned correctly for the camera angle. When Brie nodded, he returned to his submissive and murmured to her in Cheyenne. He then gave her a passionate kiss before lowering her head to protect it from the flames. Once he was satisfied that her position was safe and correct, he picked up his two floggers.

Brie waited behind the camera while Master Nosh soaked the two floggers in a bucket of isopropyl alcohol.

When he was ready, he nodded to Brie. She had Levi turned down the light.

Brie made several quick adjustments to her camera before calling out to Master Nosh that she was ready to record. She felt a thrill of excitement when he ignited the floggers and the room filled with their fiery light.

The flames danced as he approached his submissive, swinging the dual floggers in a fluid Florentine style—the burning tails flying through the air in a circular, overlapping pattern as they began grazing Nenove's bare skin with their fiery touch.

Their erotic symphony filled the entire room as the sound of one set of tails slapping her skin mixed with the sound of the other cutting through the air. Brie watched, mesmerized, as Master Nosh skillfully lashed Nenove's back with the flames, moving up and down the length of it.

Occasionally, a burst of flame would move across her back only to be snuffed out by the burning tails of the other flogger. The hypnotic aspect of the fire combined with the sensual movements of his powerful but precise strokes left Brie spellbound.

Completely captivated, Brie watched Master Nosh's graceful motions as he continued the dual flogging. He did not end the scene until the fire finally snuffed itself out.

The drummer immediately stopped, leaving them in darkened silence. But the air still resonated with the elemental energy of the scene.

Brie's heart continued to race even after Levi turned the lights back on. Awed by the magnificent scene, Brie started clapping, both in enthusiasm and out of respect for Nenove and Master Nosh.

This experience had been truly magical, and it had left Brie completely breathless.

As soon as Brie got home, she ran inside, wanting to share the experience with Sir. Her words falling all over themselves, she gushed about how incredible the scene had been to watch.

"It was amazing, Sir! I wasn't prepared for how incredible Fire Flogging really is. Watching those blazing ropes flying through the air and hearing the fire burn so fiercely as he caressed her skin with their heat…I've never seen anything more beautiful!"

She looked at him almost feverishly, unable to hide her excitement. "I can't begin to imagine what it must feel like! Unfortunately, I didn't get the chance to ask Nenove about it because Master Nosh carried her off to perform a long session of aftercare before he started his workday." She shook her head. "That poor man…"

Laughing at herself, she told him, "Here I am just babbling on and on, Sir. But I can't help it. It was just so amazing!"

"So I've heard," he chuckled.

Brie squealed and flailed her arms in excitement as she tried to describe the entire scene from start to finish. Then she suddenly remembered the children must be asleep and covered her mouth. "Hopefully, I didn't wake them…"

"No chance of that," Sir told her.

She cocked her head, a smile of understanding spreading across her lips when she saw the glint in his eyes. "They're not here, are they?"

"Correct," he answered with a sexy grin, taking her arm and guiding her toward the bedroom. "I know how excited you get after filming a scene, so I thought it might be prudent to plan a session…"

Brie let out a gasp when she walked into the room and saw a wide swath of red rose petals that had been scattered on the floor. They led to the open door of their secret room. As they walked on the path made of roses, he asked her, "Do you remember our trip to Russia, téa?"

Brie entered the room and saw that the bondage table was encircled by unlit candles set on the floor. On a small table beside it, Brie spotted all the instruments neatly set up for a session of fire play, including the fire extinguisher.

Looking up at him amorously, she answered, "I do, Master."

Sweeping his hand to the right side of the table, he said, "As you recall, the line of sadists sat in a row, waiting to enjoy our scene together."

Brie let out a little sigh, remembering how nervous she'd been that night in Russia.

Picking up a hairbrush from the table, Sir began brushing out her long hair. Chills of pleasure cascaded from her scalp down her back as he slowly stroked her hair with the bristles before binding her hair up.

Brie trembled when Sir set the brush down and guided her to the bondage table, supporting her as she stepped over the barrier of candles.

Turning her to face to the right, he murmured in her ear, "The men are watching you, téa…"

Sir began to undress her, kissing her neck as her clothes fell to the floor. Once she was completely naked, his hands roved over her breasts, teasing her as his fingers lightly pinched and tugged at her nipples.

Sir lowered his head, grazing her bare shoulder with his sensual lips. Giving in to the magic of his caress, she tapped into the memory of that night, feeding off its energy as she pretended the men in that audience were watching them.

Grinding her body against her Master, she moaned softly.

Just as he had that night, Sir lifted her right arm above her head. Running his fingers down the side of her breast, he followed the concave of her waist and the swell of her hips, tickling her skin with his light caress. Sir then picked up a long red cord. Doubling up the rope, he tied it around her right forearm, starting at the wrist, and then proceeded to create an intricate, braided pattern. When he was finished, he leaned in and murmured, "A warrior's cuff for my goddess."

Brie smiled, remembering how much it had encouraged her that night. It meant even more to her now.

He glided the fingers of one hand down her stomach and then between her thighs while he captured her breast with the other. She gasped in pleasure when she felt his fingers slide into her wet pussy.

"I knew you would be dripping wet after watching Master Nosh's skill with fire," he told her.

"I am wet, Master. So, so wet for you…"

Biting her neck lightly, he commanded, "Lie face down on the table, arms and legs outstretched."

Brie eagerly slid onto the table, moving with catlike grace, and laid herself out for him. She imagined the hungry stares of the sadists watching her.

Sir dipped a large swab into a container of alcohol, and Brie felt the welcomed coolness of it as he trailed the liquid across her skin. Sir lit a second swab and then leaned down, kissing her cheek while being careful to keep the flame away from her. "Are you ready?"

"Yes, Master."

He tapped the flame on her skin and intense heat raced up her back. Sir's hand swept the area in a fluid motion and the heat was gone.

Sir started with her back, making simple designs, then lighting them on fire before sweeping them away with his hand. Moving down to the back of her legs, he continued to do the same, even teasing the soles of her feet with the flames.

As with his undressing of her, Sir took his time, building anticipation for both Brie and their imaginary audience.

She noticed he let the flames burn longer as he advanced the scene. It required more of her concentration as the heat became deliciously intense. Repeating the words he'd said that night, he told Brie, "You and I seek the path together."

She felt him leave a trail in the shape of a spiral with the cool liquid. Brie held her breath in anticipation as he tapped it with the flame. The fire raced down the path he'd created.

Sir quickly swept it away and made a new design. This one she knew well.

"No matter what the future brings, you and I are forever connected," Sir stated as he lit the infinity symbol. Brie basked in its sensual heat and thought, *Condors forever.*

After sweeping it away, Sir then lit the ring of candles on the floor one by one before extinguishing the fire wand in his hand. He stared at her, the need in his eyes exciting her with its depth and intensity.

Sir pulled her to the edge of the table and ordered her onto her hands and knees. Stripping off his clothes, Sir caressed her bare mound tenderly before smacking her hard on the ass.

The satisfying sound of it echoed in the room, making Brie smile as she remembered the low chuckles from the men.

After cleaning his hands, Sir slid his fingers into her pussy, going straight for her G-spot. She gasped as he rolled his finger over the area slowly. Soon, her body pulsed with an insatiable need for him.

He pulled his finger out and replaced it with his shaft. She moaned hungrily when she felt his cock press against her wet opening. He thrust forcefully, filling her pussy with one solid stroke.

Dripping with desire, Brie arched her back to take his full length. Sir held nothing back as he thrust into her without restraint. She let out a primal scream, expressing her passion for him, and he met her cry with a roar of his own.

When she felt him come inside her, Brie threw her head back and allowed the excitement of the film shoot and the sexual electricity Sir had just created overwhelm her.

Brie writhed in pleasure while the powerful climax stole her breath and blurred all of her senses. It was pure submissive ecstasy.

Redemption

B rie woke up the next day with a lazy grin on her face as she listened to Hope babbling in the kitchen. Looking at the clock, she was surprised to see it was almost nine.

"That is what an epic BDSM scene will do to ya…" she purred happily to herself.

Thinking back on the night, Brie realized it had been the first scene with Sir where she had fully given herself to him without once being triggered by memories of her captivity.

By reenacting a familiar scene with her—just as he'd asked her to do with the other Doms—Sir had guided her to reconnect with those positive memories and freely embrace the entirety of the scene.

He is so damn brilliant…

Brie suddenly shot up in bed when she heard the distinct tenor of her father's voice. "What is he doing here?" she grumbled to herself as she jumped out of bed and grabbed her robe, tying the sash around herself.

Opening the door, she found her dad on the floor, playing with the children, while her mother was busy cooking in their kitchen.

Realizing Sir had asked her parents to babysit the children overnight so they could play out the scene, she glanced at him questioningly, uncertain if she was willing to deal with her father after such a wonderful night.

When her mother noticed her, she broke out in a warm smile. "Good morning, sweetie! Thane was just telling us you had a very successful shoot yesterday."

Brie smirked, still riding the high of the entire day— and the night.

Her father asked, "So, you are jumping back into the documentary?"

Brie immediately snapped at him. "Why? Do you have a problem with that, Daddy?"

He looked surprised by her tone and stammered, "No…it's remarkable you feel well enough to start so soon."

"Are you implying that you don't think I'm ready? Or are you horrified I'm going to finish another documentary about BDSM? Which is it, Daddy?" she demanded.

He shook his head. "I didn't mean it like that, little girl." Sighing, he walked up, holding his hands out to her. "I'm genuinely happy to hear it."

She looked at him doubtfully. "Why the sudden change of heart?"

Her father glanced at Sir. "I had a long talk with your husband recently. I won't lie, little girl. Your mother and I have been hurt that we haven't been a part of your lives ever since…"

"Your big blowout?" Brie finished for him, still feeling the pain of that incident.

His lips twitched, and Brie readied herself for her father to lose his cool and say something else hurtful.

He glanced nervously at Brie's mother for support, then met Brie's gaze again. "Marcy has helped me process everything Thane said to me." He frowned. "It hasn't been easy."

"What? Admitting you were wrong?" she growled.

"Brie…" Sir cautioned softly.

She glanced at Sir and sighed, knowing he was asking her to stop and listen to her father. Facing him again, Brie tried to keep the snarky tone out of her voice. "What, Daddy?"

"I'm a truthful man…it's how I'm wired," he began.

Brie folded her arms and waited impatiently, certain he was setting her up to insult again.

"I will always be uncomfortable with your 'lifestyle'. It's not something I understand and I find it extremely uncomfortable…" He gave her a hesitant smile. "However, I've come to two conclusions based on what Thane and Marcy said."

"And they are?" she prompted.

"I wouldn't have these two beautiful grandchildren…" He smiled down at Hope and Antony. "…and I wouldn't trade them for the world."

"And?" she asked, needing something more from him.

He took her hands in his. "Brianna, despite everything that's happened to you, I can see that you are happy. I would never want to steal that joy from you. Ever."

Her bottom lip trembled as she stared back at him, the lump in her throat making it impossible to speak.

"I promise I'll go to that next premier," he stated. "And, even if they throw eggs at us like they did that first time, I will stand by your side proudly."

Brie smiled and nodded, then burst out in giggles. "Thanks, Daddy…"

Brie was a bit taken by surprise when Sir informed her later that day that Marquis Gray had called.

"What did he want, Sir?" she asked in concern.

"He wants you to visit with him again."

"Don't you mean 'us', Sir?"

He shook his head. "Gray specifically stated the invitation was for you alone."

She felt her nerves kick in, and she couldn't help but think back on their last meeting. "How did he seem to you?"

"Very matter of fact."

Knitting her brow, she stated, "I'm unsure if that's a good sign or not."

"It's up to you whether you choose to go, babygirl. I want you to do what is best for you in this matter. I know you're busy with the film, and this might prove to be an unwanted distraction."

Brie understood Sir's concern, but she also knew she

could never ignore an invitation from Marquis Gray, no matter how busy she was. Setting her work aside, she went to get ready for the unexpected meet-up.

Arriving at the appointed time, Brie was not surprised to see a crowd of reporters as she pulled up to the house. Once the press had been informed the police had taken him in for questioning, they were hungry to discover why he was a person of interest.

Brie noticed Mary's car parked on the street. When she peered closer, she realized Mary was still sitting in the driver's seat. Briskly walking up to the vehicle, Brie knocked on the passenger-side window.

Mary frowned as she lowered it and snapped, "What the hell are you doing here?"

"I was about to ask you the same thing."

Glancing at the reporters, she said in a lower voice, "Marquis said he wanted to talk."

"That's what he told me, too. So, why are you still sitting in the car?"

She frowned. "You know how he is…" Mary shuddered. "I had a hard enough time dealing with Marquis's whole 'stare into your soul' gaze before. I'm not sure I can handle a darker version of that."

"Look, there's a reason he invited both of us," Brie declared, marching to the driver's side and opening the door. "And I, for one, am extremely grateful you're here."

Mary gave her a dubious look but stepped out of the car.

Taking Mary's hand for support, Brie ignored the reporters as the two of them walked up to Marquis's house. After ringing the doorbell, Mary let out an anxious sigh. "I hope we're ready for this…"

When Celestia opened the door, Mary immediately let go of Brie's hand.

"It's good to see you again," Brie told Celestia, stepping inside and giving her a hug.

After beckoning Mary inside and shutting the door, Celestia held out her arms to Mary. She hesitated for a moment before accepting the hug.

"Oh, Mary, how I've missed you!"

"Ah…sure…" Mary stammered awkwardly, giving Brie a look as if she didn't believe Celestia.

"My Master is waiting for you in the study," Celestia stated, leading them down the hallway.

Brie's anxiety increased as she stared at the closed door to the room, remembering her last meeting with Marquis.

"You first, Stinks," Mary said, pushing her toward the door.

"I'll go make us some tea," Celestia announced, glancing at Brie. "And this time, we will drink it."

Brie chuckled lightly, recalling they never had the tea when she visited last time. "I look forward to sharing a cup with you."

Grasping Mary's hand tightly, Brie dragged her toward the door and then knocked.

"Enter," she heard Marquis command.

When Brie swung the door open, she was encouraged. The lights were on, and the curtains pulled back from the window. Marquis Gray stood up from his chair as they entered the room. He moved two chairs next to his seat and invited them to sit.

Brie noticed a distinct difference in the ambiance of the room, but she was still uncertain how this meeting would go as she sat next to Mary to face him.

"I appreciate you both coming," he started. "It was important to me to have you both here today."

Brie bowed her head, telling him, "It is always an honor to see you, Marquis." When she looked up, she caught her breath. Although there was now an added layer of hardness reflected in his intense gaze, the man she knew and respected had returned.

Marquis turned his attention to Mary and explained, "I experienced a crisis of faith after I learned of your kidnapping and torture."

When Mary opened her mouth to speak, he held his hand up. Looking at both girls, he said, "I ask your forgiveness for not realizing what was happening and protecting you from Greg Holloway. While I have been reminded recently that I am not omniscient, from this point forward, I am making it my mission to be more acutely aware of individuals in positions of power, regardless of my past interactions with them."

Mary met his gaze, stating, "I never blamed you. In fact, I wanted to protect you from that fucking bastard."

He nodded slowly. "I accept the altruism behind your actions, Miss Wilson. However, I ask that in the future, rather than risk your well-being, you come directly to me with your concerns and trust I will move forward in the best interests of you and everyone involved—including myself."

Marquis glanced at Brie. "That goes for both of

you."

Brie stared into his soulful eyes and vowed solemnly, "I promise Marquis Gray."

He gave her a simple nod, then raised his eyebrow as he waited for Mary to answer.

She shook her head, telling him, "I wouldn't want you to make any sacrifices on my behalf."

"Why is that?" he asked her pointedly.

Unable to take the intensity of Marquis's gaze, Mary looked down at the floor.

"Answer me, Miss Wilson."

After several moments of silence, Brie saw teardrops falling into Mary's lap. "If given the choice, I would choose your well-being over mine every time."

"Why?" he demanded.

Mary looked up and met his gaze, holding nothing back when she said, "I'm a piece of worthless shit."

Brie gasped, crushed by Mary's disparaging words.

Marquis Gray leaned forward, never breaking eye contact with Mary. "I understand the unbearable pain of looking within yourself and seeing nothing of value—only your own depravity and an insatiable need to destroy everything around you."

She nodded, letting the tears fall unheeded.

"Miss Wilson, I found myself in that place and questioned everything I knew about myself. It was in my darkest hour that I cried out to God and received an answer."

She frowned. "I may believe in the devil, Marquis—and only because I have seen him with my own eyes—but I *definitely* do not believe in God."

"I am not asking you to," he stated firmly. "What I am telling you is that I received an answer that changed my perspective."

"How did He answer you?" she demanded. "Did the clouds part and Almighty God speak to you from the Heavens?"

He sat back, unfazed by the harsh sarcasm in her voice. "It does not matter how the message was delivered, only that I received it. I am not concerned with whether you believe me or not."

Leaning forward again, he shared with her, "In a time of profound pain and brokenness, I have come to know with unwavering certainty that He is a compassionate God."

Marquis looked at Mary with empathy. "He sees through our darkness and embraces what is good within each of us." Gazing at her tenderly, he added, "You are both, Miss Wilson—everyone is. It is up to each individual whether they choose to embrace their depravity or their virtue."

Marquis sat back and closed his eyes, sighing heavily. "I have come face to face with my insatiable rage and my capacity for evil. They are a part of me."

Opening his eyes again, Marquis stated with conviction, "After experiencing God's compassion, I have chosen to re-dedicate my life to His service."

Brie smiled with relief, confessing, "I would feel lost without your thoughtful guidance, Marquis."

Mary snorted. "You and I will never see eye to eye when it comes to God. However, I respect your decision, Marquis Gray."

He inclined his head to Mary. "I do not seek your approval. I am simply stating my truth."

Mary nodded in response.

"Please stay where you are," he ordered them both.

Marquis then stood up and walked to the door and opened it, calling for Celestia to join them.

He returned and sat back down, stating in a grave voice, "I have been thinking about the infant who was rescued from the compound."

He addressed Mary. "I've heard that the child's welfare has been weighing heavy on your mind."

New tears welled up in Mary's eyes when she nodded.

"I understand that you are burdened by the feeling that there are things you must atone for because of your involvement with Greg Holloway."

Mary's bottom lip trembled. Sounding as if she was about to break down, she answered, "Yes, I am drowning in guilt…"

"And you feel a responsibility toward that motherless child."

"I do…" she choked out.

"I feel it as well, Miss Wilson."

Mary looked up at him in surprise.

Marquis held out his hand to Celestia, who was standing in the doorway. She walked to him, a look of tenderness and devotion on her face. Taking her hand, Marquis turned to Mary. "Celestia and I have spoken at great lengths about the child. I want you to know that we are interested in petitioning to adopt him."

Mary immediately buried her face in her hands, sobs

of relief filling the room.

He continued, "You were vital in helping us care for Kaylee when Mr. Wallace traveled to Russia. If you are agreeable, we would like you to help us with this child as well. I know he will benefit from you being a part of his life as he grows up."

Mary looked up from her hands, mouthing tearfully to both of them, *Thank you.*

"There is one stipulation, however," Marquis informed her.

Grabbing the tissues that Brie had dug from her purse and handed to her, Mary asked cautiously, "What?"

"This child can act as your redemption. But it is imperative that you let go of the guilt you carry."

Mary nodded as she dabbed her eyes and sniffled.

"Miss Wilson," Marquis stated firmly.

The moment Mary met his commanding gaze, her hand froze in the act of wiping away her tears.

"You cannot bury the guilt," he insisted. "You *must* let it go."

"I don't think I can," she whimpered, her face contorting with grief.

"It serves no purpose to hold onto it. In fact, it will negatively affect the child you wish to help if you cannot let it go." He reached over and placed his hand on hers. "Do you understand that?"

Mary closed her eyes, asking in a hushed voice riddled with pain, "What if I can't, Marquis…?"

"Look at me," he stated with compassion, squeezing her hand.

When Mary opened her eyes, Marquis confessed, "I also feel responsible for every person who suffered. Therefore, you and I will hold each other accountable."

His eyes softened when he added, "You see, Miss Wilson, this child is my redemption, too."

Ultimate Role Play

B rie was so engrossed in watching the footage she'd recently shot of Master Nosh that she didn't hear Sir come up behind her until he cleared his throat.

She smiled, turning in her office chair to face him. "Is there anything you need, Sir?"

"Yes," he answered, handing her a black envelope stamped with decorative gold filigree. "This is for you," he stated formally, handing it to her.

She grinned as she turned the envelope over to open it.

"Uh-uh," he cautioned her. "You cannot open it yet."

"Oh!" Covering her mouth with excitement, she set it down on her desk. "I don't suppose you're going to tell me what this is about?"

"That is correct," he answered with a smirk.

Giggling lightly, she stared at the envelope. "When can I open it, Sir?"

"At five o'clock tonight. Not a second before then."

"What happens at five, Sir?"

"My obedient sub opens the envelope," he replied, kissing the top of her head.

"Is there anything I need to do before then?" she asked, hoping for the tiniest of hints.

"Yes," he stated matter-of-factly.

She waited anxiously for his answer.

"You must wait."

Sir picked up Hope, who was playing with blocks on the floor, and headed back down the stairs, chuckling to himself.

Brie glanced at the envelope again and then at the clock. Damn…it was going to be a long five hours.

Sir's cruelty knew no bounds.

Putting her headphones on, Brie went back to work, forcing herself not to look at the envelope for the rest of the day.

Finally, at 4:59, Brie powered down her computer and took off her headphones. Picking up the black envelope, she dutifully watched the second hand slowly tick away until it hit the appointed time. Excited, Brie broke the seal of the envelope. She pulled out a black card with the same gold print and opened it to see Sir's exquisite writing.

I read your latest entry in your journal.

Although you were unable to finish it, I have come up with a suitable ending I think you will enjoy.

Dress in the gown I have set out for you and prepare yourself just as you did in your fantasy.

A vehicle will be picking you up at seven. It will take you to the hotel I have designated. You will go to the bar to act out the rest of your fantasy.

I look forward to seeing how this plays out.

~Thane

Brie shivered in anticipation as she reread the note. Heading downstairs she noticed that the house was unusually quiet. Checking the garage, she realized that not only was Sir's car gone, but he'd arranged for childcare because she was completely alone.

Her heart racing, she headed to the bedroom and saw he had laid out a new gown on the bed. Picking up the backless dress, she grazed her hand over the black sequins sewn into the bodice. Brie smiled, knowing he had chosen this gown because it would expose the brand on her lower back. She could imagine Sir's hand grazing her skin as he traced his finger over the "T".

Sir had incredible taste in clothing, and knew how to make her feel sexy.

Brie headed to the bathroom to take a long, relaxing bath. With two hours to prepare, she took her time putting on her makeup and styling her hair. Sir had set out her Tahitian black pearls, so she finished her look by putting them on last, letting the enticingly long strand of pearls drape down against her bare back.

Brie stared thoughtfully at her reflection in the mirror. She smiled as she thought back to that young girl dressed in her Submissive Training Center uniform. That was the first time she had felt truly sexy. But looking at herself now, she realized she hadn't known what being sexy was really about.

Running her hands down her dress, Brie looked herself in the eye.

Sexy was being a mother of two, stretch marks and all, and owning the confidence that comes from surviving adversity. Sure, she'd been innocent and cute when she'd started at the Training Center, but that girl was *nothing* compared to the woman she was now.

Glancing at the clock, she grabbed her beaded clutch purse and headed out the door. She found a limousine waiting for her at the curb. Although Brie had reservations about limousines due to several bad experiences in the past, she had no doubt tonight would play out beautifully. Feeling exceedingly confident, she thanked the driver as he opened the door for her and she slipped inside.

Brie's heart raced on the drive as she imagined how the night would play out. When the driver pulled up to the Ritz-Carlton, Brie glanced up at the elegant hotel and shivered in excitement. It outclassed the hotel in her fantasy, but she loved the direction Sir was going with the scene. She could only imagine what kind of world-class clientele would be sitting at the bar.

With the driver's assistance, she stepped out of the limousine. Brie lifted her chin higher than normal and swayed her ass seductively as she stepped into the hotel lobby. It was amusing to see all the men turning their heads as she walked across the marble floor, the sexy sound of her six-inch heels catching their attention.

Knowing exactly where she was headed, Brie entered

the stylishly modern lounge and walked up to the marble-topped bar. Taking a seat, she smiled at the bartender who was handing drinks to a couple sitting farther down at the bar. He did a double take when he saw her, and in his distraction, he almost spilled the drinks he was carrying.

Hurrying to her, he asked, "You have to be a famous model. I swear I've seen you somewhere before. What's your name, gorgeous?"

Feeling mischievous, Brie pretended not to speak English and asked him a question in Italian.

He shook his head, smiling. "I have no idea what you just said, but I could listen to you talk for hours."

She smiled at him pleasantly.

In response, he asked her, "What would you like, Miss? I'll get you anything, just name it."

"*Vino rosso*," she answered, batting her eyes at him.

He grinned. "I take it you prefer Italian wine, right?"

She looked at him with a bemused smile.

Winking, he told her, "I'll get you something special, on the house, to start your evening." He left her to speak to the sommelier.

Brie took the opportunity to check out the men in the lounge. It was crowded, but she quickly found Sir. He was sitting at a table by himself, nursing a martini and looking straight at her.

The moment their eyes met, her heart skipped a beat. She quickly glanced away, in keeping with the fantasy in her journal, but it was difficult.

She was desperate to leave the bar and join him at the table. However, she wanted to play out this incredible scene he'd set up for her.

The bartender returned, and with an overly dramatic flair, placed a glass of dark red wine in front of her, telling her, "This is a 2001 Benanti Rovittello."

Brie nodded and swirled the wine several times before taking a sip. It was a dry wine with hints of flowers and ripe fruit. She set the glass down and smiled. "*Bella*," she complimented the bartender's choice.

He looked pleased. "Enjoy!"

Brie went back to scanning the men in the bar, trying to decide which one she would pick if she were really looking to hook up for a sexy one-night stand. But the truth was, no one could compare to Sir.

She glanced back at him to see he was staring at her seductively. When he picked up his martini glass and took a sip, her pussy gushed with wetness.

"Miss?" the bartender said, interrupting their silent communication.

Brie reluctantly broke Sir's gaze and turned to glance at the bartender.

"The gentleman at the other end of the bar wanted you to try this." He placed another glass of red wine in front of her.

She glanced at the end of the bar and saw a distinguished-looking businessman with salt and pepper hair.

"This is a 2004 Montevertine Il Cannaio." The bartender murmured under his breath, clearly impressed. "Over a hundred bucks per glass…"

Brie stared at the glass of wine, pretending she had no clue what he had just said, although she was equally impressed. In keeping with her journal fantasy, Brie looked at the gentleman apologetically as she gently pushed the glass back to the bartender.

The man called out in Italian, "Please enjoy, *bella donna*."

Brie gave Sir a quick glance and noticed he was wearing an amused smirk as he nodded slightly.

Understanding that this was part of the scene he'd set up, she smiled at the older gentleman, who held up his own wine glass in appreciation. Sitting back in his chair, he smiled at her with a look of satisfaction.

Realizing that both the bartender and this gentleman had been recruited by Sir for the scene, Brie smiled to herself as she swirled the glass of wine. Taking a deep sniff to appreciate the fruity aroma of the wine, she took a sip and let it play on her tongue. This wine had a blueberry taste with hints of dried fruit. She looked at the gentleman with a pleased smile. "*Delizioso*."

Brie turned to face Sir as she took a second, longer sip, not breaking his gaze. When she set the wine glass down, she turned it so he could clearly see the red impression of her lips on the glass.

To her surprise, three more gentlemen bought her drinks. Unlike the first two, she turned them down, amused by how Sir was trying to ply her with more wine than she could drink. But just like her character in the fantasy, Brie wanted to stay sober so she could enjoy every second of her time with Sir.

Just when she reached the part of her fantasy where she would get up and walk out of the bar, giving Sir an inviting glance, Brie suddenly caught the familiar combined scents of earth, spice, and leather. She immediately glanced around.

Brie stared in disbelief when she saw Rytsar walking up to the other end of the bar. He sat down and stared at her with a sexy smirk.

Her heart beat faster as she continued to stare at him, desperate to jump from the chair and run to him.

Glancing back at Sir, she gave him a questioning look, wondering what he expected her to do.

In answer, he casually picked up his glass again and took another sip.

It seemed that Sir wanted her to continue playing out the scene just as she had written it, but it was *crazy* being so close to Rytsar!

Brie could tell by the wicked glint in the Russian's eye that he was very much enjoying her current dilemma.

Fully committing to her role now, Brie slowly finished the glass of expensive wine. Between each sip, she glanced around casually, pretending to check out all the other men, but the entire time her mind was focused on Rytsar.

Once she finished the glass, Brie casually picked up her clutch and stood up. She started toward the door, glancing back at Sir, a flirtatious smile curling her lips. Walking to the elevator, Brie took out her lipstick and reapplied it with a shaking hand.

Her whole body was buzzing with excitement.

Brie recognized Sir's footsteps and, when he cleared his throat, she turned around.

"Would you be interested in dinner in my room?" he asked in a low, seductive voice.

"I would."

Sir smiled slightly as he pressed the elevator button, then guided her inside when the elevator doors opened. The moment he placed his hand on her bare back, she felt an electrical shock that traveled straight to her pussy.

Just as the doors were closing, Brie spotted Rytsar stepping out of the bar. He looked her up and down with a lustful stare.

She bit her lip, staring back at him until the doors closed, cutting him from her view. Sir took his time pressing the button for his floor and then turned to face her. He grasped Brie's chin lightly and looked deep into her eyes. "You could have any man in that room. Why did you choose only one?"

Brie smiled, enjoying the new twist he'd added to her fantasy. "I didn't want to appear too greedy," she confessed.

Pulling her to him, Sir murmured, "I understand exactly what you need." Leaning in for a kiss, he added, "I don't normally share, but for you, I would."

Brie moaned softly, responding to his touch just as the elevator slowed to a stop on the second floor. The two of them turned away from each other and stared straight ahead, pretending not to know each other when the elevator doors opened.

Brie could barely contain herself when it was Rytsar who stepped into the elevator. He gave her a sideways glance, that wicked smirk returning to his face.

Once the elevator doors closed, both men descended on her. Rytsar grabbed the back of her neck, kissing her lustfully, while Sir pressed his body against her from behind, grabbing her waist. Brie felt the strength of Sir's erection, and her nipples hardened achingly in response to the intimate contact of both men.

Brie gave in to Rytsar's fiery kisses while Sir explored her body roughly with his hands. She moaned, entranced by the intense chemistry the three of them shared. But then, Brie was disappointed when she felt the elevator slow again.

The three broke away from each other and stared straight ahead as the doors opened again. Two women entered the elevator and eyed Rytsar and Sir up and down lustfully, completely ignoring Brie. She noticed the two sharing a covert smile. They looked as if they were silently hatching a plan to snag her men.

A smile crept across Brie's lips as she stood there observing them.

When the elevator continued upward, Brie felt Sir's finger on her lower back as he lightly traced it over her brand. His electric touch caused her pussy to contract in pleasure, and she had to bite her lip to keep from moaning out loud.

When the elevator stopped at the next floor, Sir stepped out and Rytsar immediately followed. Not about to be left behind, Brie walked out of the elevator with them and turned around, waving demurely at the two women as the doors closed.

My Heart

S ir stopped at the last suite at the end of the long hallway. After unlocking the door, he opened it and looked at Brie, saying with a seductive smile, "Ladies first."

Brie glanced at both men, her arousal off the charts as she walked into the spacious suite. The white décor was elegant and modern, with a silver leaf design accenting the walls throughout the room. But her eyes were naturally drawn to the large California King bed.

Once all three were inside, Sir closed the door and asked Brie, "Do you like my addition to your fantasy?"

She nodded, then turned to grin at Rytsar. "I can't believe this!"

"Here in the flesh," Rytsar announced, grabbing the back of her neck to give her another passionate kiss. When he pulled away, she was left breathless.

Staring at him in pleasant disbelief, Brie asked, "I thought you weren't coming back for a while."

He smirked. "I didn't want to spoil the surprise, *ra-*

dost moya."

She shook her head as she looked at both of them. "Well, you definitely surprised me!"

"How should we proceed, *moy droog*?" Rytsar asked.

"Tonight is a night of celebration," Sir stated, placing his hand on Rytsar's shoulder. "We celebrate your return and the safe capture of Lilly."

Rytsar nodded and glanced over at Brie. "If the good doctor can treat the creature, all the better, but the creature cannot cause harm again."

She threw her arms around him, overcome with relief. "Thank you from the very depths of my soul."

He gazed at her with those intense blue eyes. "Now you can concentrate fully on your future, *radost moya.*"

She nodded, tears of gratitude welling up.

"No tears tonight," he admonished her, then added with a wicked grin, "Unless I cause them."

Turning to Sir, he said, "When you say celebration, I assume vodka is involved."

"Of course," he chuckled, opening a cabinet stocked with fine alcohol. Sir took out three shot glasses and picked up the bottle of Zyr from the selection.

While he was filling them, Brie asked, "Sir, why did you have so many men send me drinks? Were you trying to get me drunk?"

He stopped pouring for a moment and laughed. "I had nothing to do with that."

"Really?" Brie exclaimed in surprise.

Sir nodded as he went back to pouring. "Those were genuine attempts to garner your favor."

She shook her head, murmuring, "But there were so

many…!"

"You do look particularly enchanting tonight, *radost moya*," Rytsar stated, looking her over with an approving eye.

She blushed at his compliment.

"I agree with Durov," Sir said, studying her. "It's more than the dress or the makeup. There is an alluring energy radiating from you tonight."

Brie loved that he'd noticed and told Sir, "I feel like I've fully come into my own."

His smile was captivating. "It is a beautiful sight, babygirl."

Moved by his words, she blushed a deeper shade of pink.

Sir handed the first shot glass to Rytsar and gave Brie the second, holding up his own in a toast. In a gruff voice, he told Rytsar, "I'm eternally grateful to you, brother."

"We are one, brother," Rytsar replied in a somber tone. "Gratitude is unnecessary."

Grinning at Brie, Rytsar stated, "Therefore, I will start off the evening's celebration with a proper Russian toast." Holding his glass high, he shouted, "Tonight, let our tables break from abundance and our beds break from love!"

"Let the breaking commence!" Brie giggled as she clinked glasses with both of them.

Rytsar poured another round of vodka. After downing the shot, he placed his hand on the back of her neck and squeezed. His dominant hold made her feel weak in the knees.

"Shall we begin?" Sir asked him.

Brie felt butterflies as both men silently undressed her. The two covered her in kisses as they removed each piece of clothing, leaving her naked and trembling with desire once they were done.

"I have longed to touch you again," Rytsar growled, grazing her pussy with his fingers.

Sir kept her captivated by his sensual kisses and teased her with his tongue. When Rytsar began vigorously rubbing her sensitive clit, she moaned, swaying unsteadily on her feet. She squealed in surprise when Rytsar suddenly swept her off her feet and carried her to the bed.

Brie looked up at both men as she lay there, craving a deeper connection with each of them. Holding her hands out to both, she begged, "Lay with me."

With ravenous looks of desire, the two men undressed in front of her. Brie openly stared at their bodies. She admired Rytsar's muscular body, covered in old scars, and his signature dragon tattoo with the smoke swirling from its mouth that had been artfully added to spell out the words *"radost moya"*.

Her gaze then drifted to Sir's masculine body. She loved the dark hair that not only covered his toned chest and powerful thighs but framed his rigid shaft. Of all the men she'd ever seen, Sir's cock was the most handsome of all.

"*Radost moya*, let your men love you," Rytsar murmured huskily, joining her on the bed and claiming her lips while Sir positioned himself between her legs.

Brie closed her eyes, her heart bursting with love as

they pleased and teased her body. Thoroughly enjoying their dual attention, she ran her hands over Rytsar's muscular back.

Stiffening, her breath suddenly caught. "Wait!"

Both men pulled away from her with concern in their eyes.

She frowned at Rytsar. "What happened?"

He chuckled and reached back to rub the hard ridge of stitches. "It's nothing."

"What is Brie talking about?" Sir demanded.

Rolling his eyes in exasperation, Rytsar twisted his torso to show Sir his injury and stated, "It's just a scratch."

"That's no scratch," Sir growled. "It looks like a stab wound."

Brie sat up to look at the wound more closely. Tracing the line of ugly black stitches, she cried, "Did Lilly do this?"

"Stop," Rytsar barked at both of them. "I'm fine."

Looking at Brie, he assured her, "I was never in danger."

"This looks dangerous to me," she protested as she stared at the wound.

"We will speak about it later," he insisted, his command harsh.

Rytsar sighed deeply and turned to Sir. "*This* is what I need right now, brother."

Sir looked at him with concern but, after several seconds, he nodded. "So be it, Anton."

"Good," Rytsar proclaimed in satisfaction.

Gazing deep into Brie's eyes, Rytsar said the one

thing that could melt away all of her defenses. "Make love to your warrior."

Responding to his need, Brie momentarily pushed her concern for him to the side and obeyed. Lying back down, she grasped his cock and gave it a light kiss before taking it into her mouth. She looked up at him lovingly as she encased the head of it with her lips.

Rytsar watched her, groaning in pleasure as she slowly took his length into her mouth. Letting out a low growl, he grabbed her head and guided her to take even more of his shaft.

Brie consciously relaxed her throat so she could take him deeper. When the Russian grunted in satisfaction, Brie felt tingles race through her. Encouraged by his response, she took her time lavishing her love on his cock. Soon, however, her thighs began to shake uncontrollably as Sir skillfully caressed her G-spot, coaxing an orgasm from her.

Turned on by the sounds of her wet excitement, Rytsar growled hungrily, "I must claim you, *radost moya*."

She and Sir were now painfully aware of Rytsar's wound. As a result, Sir lay down on the bed and pulled Brie on top of him, so she was straddling his pelvis. "I want to feel that wet pussy covering my shaft, *téa*."

Brie longed for the feeling of his cock inside her, and slowly lowered herself onto his rigid shaft, mewing softly as she took his length and then ground her pussy against him.

She turned her head to watch as Rytsar stroked his cock, covering it with lubricant from a vial he had brought. He smiled at her wickedly as he wiped his hands with a towel.

"Look at me," Sir commanded.

Brie stared into her Master's passionate eyes while Rytsar positioned himself behind her. She let out a little gasp when she felt the head of Rytsar's shaft open her up as he breached her tight entrance.

"Take all of me, *radost moya*," Rytsar growled in a low voice, grabbing her waist as he slowly pushed himself deeper inside her. She loved the aching challenge of taking the two men at once and moaned with desire.

Rytsar leaned forward and bit her flesh, causing her to cry out. He then left a fiery trail of bite marks down her back. At the same time, Sir grabbed her breasts and squeezed them. She purred when she felt the warmth of his mouth encasing her nipple before he began sucking hard.

Every lick, suck, and stroke was building her toward another orgasm.

Normally more aggressive with his passion, Rytsar was slow and patient as he opened her up with steady strokes. Her pussy gushed with wetness as she gave in to the intense sensation of taking both cocks deeply.

Brie bit her bottom lip. Even though she had taken them this way countless times before, she still had to force her body to relax in order to receive their double penetration. It was part of the reason she enjoyed it so much.

The act required her total submission, and the connection it created between the three of them was like nothing else in the world.

The two men moved in tandem as they increased the

power of each stroke. Brie moaned in painful pleasure as she received their dual love. Together, the two men rocked her body with their unbridled passion.

Rytsar roared in pleasure, tightening his hands around her waist.

Brie looked down at Sir. His eyes flashed with ravenous need when he ordered, "Come for your men, téa."

Throwing her head back, Brie let out a cry of sheer ecstasy as she embraced their intense love. A powerful rush overtook her as she climaxed for them.

Both men groaned in unison as Brie felt the heat of their lustful releases as they came inside her.

Afterward, the room fell quiet.

In the silence that followed, Brie slowly disengaged from them and showered their bodies with kisses, wanting to express with her lips the depth of the love she felt in her heart. She then lay back down between them, content.

"This is only the beginning," Sir informed her, leaning over to use the hotel phone.

Picking up the receiver, he stated, "Please send up my order in thirty minutes."

Setting it back down, Sir turned to her. "I did promise you a meal, didn't I?"

Brie giggled. "You did, Sir."

After a quick shower, Brie insisted on dressing both men. By the time their meal arrived, the three of them were sitting in the lounge area, sipping on the martinis Sir had made.

When room service knocked, Rytsar insisted on answering the door. Two gentlemen entered the room and laid out a large number of covered plates on the dining table.

But before they left, one of them handed Brie a single red rose with a note attached. The man bowed to her before leaving the room.

Intrigued, Brie smelled the rose to take in its sweet scent, before reading the note.

Beneath the flames of desire, my heart beats for you.

~Thane

She turned to him at a loss for words.

Looking at her tenderly, Sir leaned forward and swept a lock of hair from her face. "Condors forever, babygirl."

I hope you enjoyed ***Beneath the Flames!***

Reviews mean the world to me.

COMING UP NEXT

Craving His Touch:

Brie's Submission Book 26

(April 2023)

This next part of Brie's journey is going to steal your breath away.

Get ready for some deliciously wicked fun

Sign up and read the EXCLUSIVE SCENE

that is smoking hot with Sir, Brie, Lea, and Hunter! 🩶

COMING NEXT
Craving His Touch
Brie's Submission Book 26
Available for Preorder

EXCLUSIVE BONUS SCENE FOR YOU!

Read the scorching hot scene between Sir, Brie, Lea, and Hunter on the cruise ship that didn't make it into the book.

Read it now by going to this link to sign up to my newsletter: https://geni.us/BTFBonusChapter

Get the sexy scene NOW!

If you are already signed up, go to the same link!

Reviews mean the world to me, my friend 💚

I truly appreciate you taking the time to review ***Beneath the Flames***.

ABOUT THE AUTHOR

Over Two Million readers have enjoyed Red's stories

Red Phoenix – USA Today Bestselling Author
Winner of 8 Readers' Choice Awards

Hey Everyone!

I'm Red Phoenix, an author who also happens to be a submissive in real life. I wrote the Brie's Submission series because I wanted people everywhere to know just how much fun BDSM can be.

There is a huge cast of characters who are part of Brie's journey. The further you read into the story the more you learn about each one. I hope you grow to love Brie and the gang as much as I do.

They've become like family.

When I'm not writing, you can find me online with readers.

I heart my fans! ~Red

To find out more visit my Website

redphoenixauthor.com

Follow Me on BookBub

bookbub.com/authors/red-phoenix

Newsletter: Sign up

redphoenixauthor.com/newsletter-signup

Facebook: AuthorRedPhoenix

Twitter: @redphoenix69

Instagram: RedPhoenixAuthor

I invite you to join my reader Group!

facebook.com/groups/539875076052037

SIGN UP FOR MY NEWSLETTER
HERE FOR THE LATEST RED
PHOENIX UPDATES

FOLLOW ME ON INSTAGRAM
INSTAGRAM.COM/REDPHOENIXAUTHOR

SALES, GIVEAWAYS, NEW
RELEASES, PREORDER LINKS,
AND MORE!
SIGN UP HERE
REDPHOENIXAUTHOR.COM/NEWSLETTER-
SIGNUP

Red Phoenix is the author of:

Brie's Submission Series:
Teach Me #1

Love Me #2

Catch Me #3

Try Me #4

Protect Me #5

Hold Me #6

Surprise Me #7

Trust Me #8

Claim Me #9

Enchant Me #10

A Cowboy's Heart #11

Breathe with Me #12

Her Russian Knight #13

Under His Protection #14

Her Russian Returns #15

In Sir's Arms #16

Bound by Love #17

Tied to Hope #18

Hope's First Christmas #19

Secrets of the Heart #20

Her Sweet Surrender #21

The Ties That Bind #22

A Heart Unchained #23

Whispered Promises #24

Beneath the Flames #25

Craving His Touch #26

*You can also purchase the AUDIO BOOK **Versions**

Also part of the Submissive Training Center world:

Rise of the Dominates Trilogy
Sir's Rise #1
Master's Fate #2
The Russian Reborn #3

Captain's Duet
Safe Haven #1
Destined to Dominate #2

Unleashed Series
The Russian Unleashed #1
The Cowboy's Secret #2
Sir's Destiny #3

Other Books by Red Phoenix

Blissfully Undone
* Available in eBook and paperback

(Snowy Fun—Two people find themselves snowbound
in a cabin where hidden love can flourish, taking one
couple on a sensual journey into ménage à trois)

His Scottish Pet: Dom of the Ages
* Available in eBook and paperback

Audio Book: *His Scottish Pet: Dom of the Ages*

(Scottish Dom—A sexy Dom escapes to Scotland in the
late 1400s. He encounters a waif who has the potential to
free him from his tragic curse)

The Only One
* Available in eBook and paperback

(Sexual Adventures—Fate has other plans but he's not letting her go…she is the only one!)

Passion is for Lovers
* Available in eBook and paperback

(Super sexy novelettes—*In 9 Days, 9 Days and Counting, And Then He Saved Me*, and *Play With Me at Noon*)

Varick: The Reckoning
* Available in eBook and paperback

(Savory Vampire—A dark, sexy vampire story. The hero navigates the dangerous world he has been thrust into with lusty passion and a pure heart)

eBooks

Keeper of the Wolf Clan (Keeper of Wolves, #1)

(Sexual Secrets—A virginal werewolf must act as the clan's mysterious Keeper)

The Keeper Finds Her Mate (Keeper of Wolves, #2)

(Second Chances—A young she-wolf must choose between old ties or new beginnings)

The Keeper Unites the Alphas (Keeper of Wolves, #3)

(Serious Consequences—The young she-wolf is captured
by the rival clan)

Boxed Set: Keeper of Wolves Series (Books 1-3)

(Surprising Secrets—A secret so shocking it will rock
Layla's world. The young she-wolf is put in a position of
being able to save her werewolf clan or becoming the
reason for its destruction)

Socrates Inspires Cherry to Blossom

(Satisfying Surrender—A mature and curvaceous woman
becomes fascinated by an online Dom who has much to
teach her)

By the Light of the Scottish Moon

(Saving Love—Two lost souls, the Moon, a werewolf,
and a death wish…)

Play With Me at Noon

(Seeking Fulfillment—A desperate wife lives out her
fantasies by taking five different men in five days)

CPSIA information can be obtained
at www.ICGtesting.com
Printed in the USA
BVHW041121060423
661869BV00014B/559